3

HIS TORMENTED HEART

AN ISLAND OF YS NOVEL

KATEE ROBERT

TRINKETS AND TALES LLC

ALSO BY KATEE ROBERT

Book 3: Protecting Fate

Come Undone Series
Book 1: Wrong Bed, Right Guy
Book 2: Chasing Mrs. Right
Book 3: Two Wrongs, One Right
Book 3.5: Seducing Mr. Right

Other Books
Seducing the Bridesmaid
Meeting His Match
Prom Queen
The Siren's Curse

CONTENT WARNING

This book contains depictions of a character with a history of abuse (off-page).

CHAPTER 1

*R*yu shouldn't be in the club. There were a thousand and one things to handle, and double that number he couldn't bear thinking about. After the events of the last couple weeks, he didn't know if the Horsemen were planning an assassination ... or a war. And, because he didn't know, because the truth of their enemy shredded him to pieces again and again over every waking hour, this was where he gravitated to. This was *who* he gravitated to.

To Delilah.

To watch her dance.

She moved around the stage as if she owned it, as comfortable in a tiny thong as most people were fully clothed. Her dancing ...

It defied description. Strength and beauty and a very specific kind of power. Each motion radiated it to the extreme. Add in the gravity-defying moves she pulled off with ease on the pole and Ryu was like every other person in this place.

Captivated.

Enraptured.

Most importantly, *distracted*.

When he watched Delilah spin her web of desire through the room, he wasn't thinking about the next step in their plan. He wasn't going damn near cross-eyed from yet another hour on the computer, looking for answers Ryu wasn't sure existed. And he sure as fuck wasn't dealing with the truth that had set fire to whatever he thought he knew of this world.

In the darkness of the corner booth, he could be anyone. Some random rich asshole who patronized the Island. The kind of man who hadn't a care beyond where he'd make his next million.

She regained her feet lifted her arms over her head, putting her body on full display. Her light brown skin glowed with perspiration, leading the mind to all kinds of filthy fucking. Small, high breasts with brown nipples gone taunt in the icy air conditioning. Muscles moved with every sway, belying the strength and training it took to do what she did. A white lacy thong which almost, *almost* gave a glimpse of her pussy.

Ryu forced himself to lean back, to breath the tension from his body, but he couldn't look away as she twisted and bent at the waist, putting her ass on display in a way that made his breath catch.

Every. Single. Time.

And then it was over. The music trailed away and she gave a brilliant smile which seemed like it was only for him. A final wave and she sauntered off the stage, ignoring the piles of cash the other customers threw at her. One of the other employees would come pick it up before the next set and deliver it to her backstage.

Ryu reached for his drink with a hand that shook, just a little. He didn't pick up the glass, didn't need more alcohol.

He'd had more than normal tonight. Not just tonight. Every night since the day they learned the name of their enemy.

Fai Zhao.

Or, as Ryu and Amarante knew him—Father.

He shuddered and grabbed the glass, downing the rest of the scotch, wishing it could burn away his memories the same way it burned his throat. Ten years of his childhood filled with pain and suffering beyond comprehension. Another fifteen spent planning their revenge. Only to discover the person who put them in that hellhole was their own goddamn father.

He hadn't come to terms with that truth. Ryu didn't think a person *could* come to terms with a truth that reprehensible. So here he came, night after night, seeking out the one thing that lightened the weight he carried.

Delilah.

A woman he hadn't exchanged two words with. One who didn't even know his real name. One employed by the Horsemen. Three very good reasons to turn around and leave. To find something else to do on the nights when the truth rode him too hard. *Every night.*

He didn't leave.

He never left.

Instead, Ryu finished his drink and climbed to his feet. This was his chance to make the right choice, to head back to his rooms and sleep off the sick feeling in his chest. He didn't go back to his rooms. He never did. Instead, he headed for the private dancing rooms they had situated around the club.

Technically, club wasn't the right word. The business was part of Pleasure, one of the two casinos the Island of Ys hosted. Outside this darkened room, there were a thousand and one ways to gamble and drink and fuck your way out of a truly absurd amount of money. Most of that profit went

3

into the Horsemen's pockets, but they ensured that their people were paid and paid well.

The dancers at this club didn't have sex with customers. If the people lingering on the darkened floor, waiting for the next show, wanted the sort of entertainment that came with touching privileges, there were other places in Pleasure to have

their needs met. Similarly, if the dancers wanted to indulge, it was arranged as required. There were rules for a reason.

Rules that he broke every time he came here.

Oh, none of his siblings gave a fuck if he liked to watch the dancers strip, to watch one particular dancer. They each had their own ways of quieting the memories, one of the things they rarely spoke about. No, it was Ryu's own rules that should have kept him from walking through the door.

The second his attraction to Delilah flared to life, he *should* have put a stop to it. And when he realized he preferred watching her to anyone else in this place?

If he had anything left resembling a soul, that would have warned him off.

And yet here he was, walking into Delilah's private dancing room. The rooms weren't large, but they held enough space for a curved couch which could fit a few people and a small round stage and pole. That was it.

The lights dimmed, giving him half a breath to school his expression before *she* walked into the room. In the time since she'd left the stage, she'd changed into his favorite outfit. It was a short black dress that appeared to be made of nothing but beaded strings. With every move, it revealed swathes of skin. The strings covering her breasts were spaced wide enough that he could see her nipples, and she'd pulled her hair up into a high ponytail. Delilah stepped onto the stage on sky-high heels and gave him a surprisingly sweet smile. "The usual?"

Ryu nodded. He never spoke during these illicit dances. Bad enough that he was here. For all intents and purposes, he was her boss. That should be enough to keep him away on its own. Add in the sheer amount of baggage Ryu carted around and it was a lost cause. A conversation, even a short one, opened the door to him dirtying this woman. She deserved better than that.

She sure as fuck deserved better than to be his life raft, too.

Music ground through the speakers cleverly hidden around the room, a slow, grinding melody that Delilah picked up effortlessly. She ignored the pole for the time being, simply rolling her hips and letting her body move to the beat. In moments like this, Ryu had no doubt that she loved dancing as much as he loved watching. Not *because* he was watching. She loved dancing for the sake of dancing. It was written in every move she made as she circled the pole once, twice, a third time, and went to her knees facing away from him. She spread her legs and kept up that delicious rolling of her hips. Because the couch was several inches shorter than the stage, he could see her lace panties, the scrap of fabric barely enough to cover her. The curves of her ass …

Fuck.

Ryu dragged a hand over his face. If he was going to insist on doing this, he should at least keep his shit on lock. It never happened, though. She bent over and he lost control of his blank expression.

Every. Single. Time.

Delilah worked her way around to face him and straightened enough to grasp the hem of that sad excuse for a dress. Her dancing had parted the beads farther, her breasts now fully on display. She tilted her head to the side. "Would you like me to take it off?"

Even though he knew this was a game to her, that she gave this show to anyone who paid the high premium, his mouth went dry as he nodded slowly. He forced his hands to relax as she worked the dress slowly up her body and over her head. And then it was gone, leaving her in only the panties. She bit her bottom lip as if debating with herself, and finally climbed off the stage.

Ryu froze.

This wasn't part of the show.

Delilah moved to stand between his knees. The position left her breasts level with his face, so close he could see the way her nipples peaked under his gaze and goosebumps spread across her skin. She stopped before she closed that last bit of distance between them. "Can I ask you a question … Pestilence?"

Pestilence.

Each of Ryu's siblings had taken a moniker of one of the Four Horsemen when they founded the Island of Ys. It may have started as their own private joke—a marker of their determination to bring a very personal apocalypse to their enemies—but over the years their reputations had become something else altogether. They evolved into a kind of living legend that made all sorts of people sit up and take notice. People might not look twice at Ryu, but they worked hard not to piss off Pestilence. Everyone knew what he could do, how he could make people disappear without ever laying a finger on them. He might not be the most violent of his siblings, but aside from Death, he was the one people whispered about most.

Delilah lifted a dark brow, and he realized he was staring instead of answering her question. Finally, he nodded. She gave a small smile. "I've worked here for two years, and the

only time I've seen you around is in the last three weeks ...
when you started coming every single night."

There wasn't a question in there, so Ryu leaned back and
propped his arms on the couch. Waiting.

"Every night, you come in here and watch me dance, and
every night you book a private dance immediately after."

Still no question.

Her hand drifted down to his chest. The second her
fingers pressed against him, his lungs turned to concrete. He
couldn't breathe, couldn't think, couldn't do more than
grapple with the instinct to fight or flee. If he didn't do
something *right now*, the pain would come. It always came
after a stranger touched him ...

Delilah made a pained squeak, and Ryu blinked at his
hand gripping her wrist tightly enough to have her fingers
splayed. He released her instantly and she staggered back to
sit on the stage. Shit.

Shit. Shit. *Shit.*

He needed to apologize. Needed to explain that he didn't
like being touched, especially not here in this room that
suddenly reeked of fucking. He inhaled and he could taste
the scent on his tongue. Even though he knew it was all in
his head, he couldn't get the smell out of his nose, his mouth,
his throat.

Oh fuck, I'm going to puke.

Ryu shoved to his feet and stalked out of the room. He
couldn't think, couldn't plan, couldn't do anything but move.
He barely made it to the bathroom down the hall in time to
lose every bit of the alcohol he'd just consumed. His stomach
heaved again and again, leaving him lightheaded and woozy.

Not woozy enough to forget what just happened.

He stumbled to the sink and splashed water on his face.
He needed to go apologize to Delilah. But as he looked at his
haunted eyes in the mirror, Ryu had to admit if he sought her

out again, he couldn't guarantee his control would hold. He wouldn't hurt her again. He'd cut off his fucking hand before he did. But stringing words together into coherent sentences?

No.

The past twisted too close to the surface to trust himself completely. He wouldn't find the right words. Odds were that he'd actually make it worse. Ryu pulled a hand towel out of the basket and carefully wiped his face. He didn't have the control to smooth his expression out right now, but it'd have to do until he could get back to the hub. One deep breath to fortify himself and he pushed out of the bathroom and stalked down the hall.

He couldn't handle the thought of being alone right now, and if Ryu wasn't currently capable of making amends, one of his siblings would have to do it. He ducked through one of the doors that led to the warren of private hallways that wove through Pleasure's core. Many of them were used by staff to move about unseen, but a good portion were for Horsemen use alone. Ten minutes later, he walked into the central hub where he and his siblings kept their private rooms and hesitated.

Not Kenzie. She was the sister of his heart, if not his blood. She might understand better than any of them why he reacted the way he did, but these days she didn't room alone. Seeing her partner, Liam, having to explain to someone who hadn't *been there* … He couldn't do it.

He veered right toward Amarante's suite, and barged through the door without knocking. His sister sat at her desk wearing shorts and a tank top, her long black hair piled in a knot on her head. She wasn't messy enough to have come from the gym, so she must be heading there after she finished whatever she was working on.

She looked up. Her eyes widened the tiniest bit, the only tell she'd allow, even with him. "What happened?"

"I fucked up."

Amarante pushed to her feet and pointed at the chair she'd just vacated. "Sit. Now."

"Te—"

"Sit down before you fall down." She strode behind him to the door and closed it softly. Once he stumbled to the chair and sank onto it, she crouched in front of him. "You went to the club again."

Of course she knew where he went when he disappeared from the hub. Amarante knew everything that went down on the island. "It's the only place I can think."

She chose not to comment on that, which he appreciated. Instead she sat back on her heels and studied him. "Tell me."

"She touched me."

Understanding flared in Amarante's dark eyes. "Ah." She hesitated the briefest of seconds. "How badly did you hurt her?"

He should feel grateful that his sister understood. Ryu didn't feel grateful. He felt like the biggest piece of shit in existence. Amarante hadn't hesitated. She obviously trusted his control just as little as he did. "Bruises, I think. I snapped out of it quickly."

"Ah," she said again. Amarante pushed to her feet. "I'll take care of it."

Knowing her, that could mean a medic—or a coroner. "Te."

She stopped by the door. "Yes?"

"It wasn't her fault."

"Did you ask her to touch you?"

So deadly, his sister. He took a breath and forced the shake out of his tone. Amarante rose to meet any perceived threat to their little family with a viciousness that was the

9

main reason their legend had grown at an exponential rate in the last five years. Of course she wouldn't see this as a sin on Ryu's shoulders. He hurt Delilah, but she broke the rules and caused him distress in the process.

Amarante would squash her like a bug.

"It wasn't her fault," he repeated. "I don't want her punished for my ..." What to even call it? His fractured soul. The baggage he carried around the same way Atlas carried the world. If he asked his other sister, she'd be able to rattle off half a dozen amusing terms without pausing to think. Quippy shit had never been Ryu's strong suit. He didn't need pretty words to define his issues. They existed, and that was enough.

Again, something in his sister softened the tiniest bit. "You like her."

Just like that, his feet were on steady ground again. If there was anything worse than Amarante on a warpath, it was her deciding to meddle. He pushed slowly to his feet and took a breath. "It doesn't matter. You know that better than most. Even if we didn't have all this shit bearing down on us, that kind of thing is off limits for me."

"Kenzie and Luca found people."

"It's different for them and you know it." When Kenzie arrived in that camp, Ryu and Amarante had already been there five years. By the time they escaped, the clock showed an entire decade. A decade of abuse and horror and the kind of damage adults didn't bounce back from.

Ryu was *five* when they were stolen from their family.

He almost laughed at the thought. Stolen from their family. The lie he always believed, what they'd both believed. The narrative he'd clung to for twenty-five years no longer held water. Impossible to be stolen from your family when *your father* ran the organization responsible. He closed his eyes. Maybe there would come a day when that truth didn't knife him in the gut, but it wouldn't happen while that bastard walked this earth. "We have to kill him."

"By all rights, we should burn our bloodline to ash and scatter it to the wind."

He opened his eyes. "Te, the Zhao bloodline numbers in the hundreds when you take in the extended family tree."

She shrugged. "How many of them are receiving funds drenched in the blood of children?"

"Seventy-two." He knew because he'd tracked the money. Child's play once they had a target to focus on. Ryu spent two weeks straight confirming that Fai Zhao was, in fact, responsible. Two weeks of digging through their father's finances, of finding shell corporations within shell corporations, before he finally tugged on the right string and it led him to the truth. In the seven days since then, he'd dug deep to find out how far the rot spread.

The whole family was tainted by benefit. The question remained how many of them were tainted by knowledge. "We would have those funds, too, if we were still there."

"We're not. He made sure of that." Cold fury rolled off Amarante in waves. "And if we *had* stayed, then we'd deserve to be punished, too."

He ran his hands over his face. "We have the evidence. We know where he is. Why aren't we moving on him?"

"He's too well protected. I haven't found a way in yet." The same thing his sister had said the last dozen times he asked her. "When I do, you'll be the first to know."

"Te—"

"This isn't easy for me, either." She glanced at the door. "I haven't … I don't know how we're going to play this, yet. He's got everything locked up so tightly, it's creating some difficult challenges."

Something there beneath her surface, something deeper than grappling with the fact their father was the kind of monster only found in horror stories. Amarante didn't falter, and she didn't waffle. Not once she'd set herself on a course of action. Every plan put into place, every step they'd taken to work their way closer and closer to the truth … She never once showed the hesitation now written in her eyes.

He frowned. "What else is going on?"

"I'm not ready to talk about it." Confirmation enough that something else *was* going on. She gave him a pained smile. "We'll get through this, just like we've gotten through everything. Together."

In the end, that's all he could ask for. His blood might be tainted, but the only family that truly mattered was the four of them. Ryu just had to hold to that truth, no matter how shaky the foundation beneath his feet. He matched her pained smile. "Together."

CHAPTER 2

*D*elilah didn't miscalculate. Too many times in the past, her very life had depended on the ability to read another person and react accordingly. Her *sister's* life had depended on it.

She grimaced at the bruises blossoming under the skin of her wrist. A mistake, and a costly one. She tentatively opened and closed her hand. Nothing was damaged, but she needed all her strength to accomplish the pole moves in her routine. Plus, the fantasy the stage created didn't include bruised and damaged women. The manager told her to take a week off, and it wasn't a suggestion. A freaking *week*.

All because she couldn't keep her hands to herself.

You know why.

Her gaze tracked to the phone she wasn't supposed to have. The Island of Ys—the Horsemen—had strict rules for their employees. In return, they paid out an absurd amount in payroll and protected their people. Not to mention the added bonus of living and working in paradise. Except these days, it didn't feel much like paradise for Delilah.

It felt like a trap clamped around her thigh.

The phone had appeared in her room a week ago, and the memory of the first call still had her breaking out in a cold sweat. A man who delivered threats as easily as breathing, never once raising his voice. Threatening *Esther* if Delilah didn't follow his exact instructions. When Delilah called his bluff ... the pictures of her sister started pinging through.

Esther in class at Columbia.

Esther studying while she ate dinner at the little restaurant she loved so much.

Esther sleeping *in her bed*.

The last one convinced Delilah that the threats were anything but empty. He could get to her baby sister, and he could do it whenever he wanted. She had no choice but to agree to his terms.

Find out everything she could about the Horsemen who rule the Island of Ys. An impossible task.

In the two years she'd worked here, she'd personally interacted with exactly two of them. War handled her interview and then got her set up in both work and housing. Delilah liked the blond woman, liked her brazen, flirty nature, even though the promise of violence beneath the surface left her wary of getting too close.

And the other?

Pestilence.

She gingerly touched her wrist. All the Horsemen were dangerous. It was a fact of life on the island. They might reward loyalty to a truly absurd financial degree, but when people stepped out of line, the response was quick and brutal.

Impossible to see what happened in the private room as anything but that. A punishment. She broke the rules, and he'd responded in kind. She should probably consider herself lucky. Word was that people who pissed Pestilence off woke up the next day with no bank account and no social security number. He didn't have to kill them to make them disappear, and his way almost seemed more cruel.

Now *she'd* gone and pissed him off. She gave a hoarse laugh. "A mistake." One she couldn't afford to make.

A knock on her door had her scrambling to shove the phone beneath her mattress. She didn't know what would happen if they found it in her room. Expulsion from the island, minimum. If they found out what the person on the other end of the line demanded Delilah do?

Worse.

So much worse.

She pushed to her feet on wobbly legs and tied her robe more firmly around her waist. *Just breathe. You know how to do this. It's just pretend, just for a little while.* She took one final breath, smoothed out her frown into a neutral expression, and opened the door.

Death stood on the other side.

Rumor had it the Horsemen were siblings, but Death and Pestilence were the only ones who looked related by blood. They were both Chinese, remote, and painfully beautiful. Death wore a simple suit tonight—if a person didn't know enough about expensive clothing to know better. It was gray and fitted her lean body perfectly. Her black hair hung in a curtain, and her make-up was, as always, on point. Subtle eyes and bold red lips.

She studied Delilah for a few moments. "Let me see."

No point in pretending to misunderstand. Pestilence had harmed her, now Death was here to judge the situation. The fact it was Death and not War ... No use thinking about that. Not if she wanted to maintain her composure.

Delilah tentatively held out her arm. "I shouldn't have touched him."

"He lost control." Death took her hand and gently

explored the bruise. "But you're right—you shouldn't have touched him. It's against the rules, Delilah."

The way Death said her name sounded like a threat. She swallowed hard. "I know. I'm sorry."

"Have you seen the doctor on staff?"

"No." She fought the urge to yank her hand out of Death's grasp. "If it had been someone else … But I didn't want to cause problems." She didn't even tell her manager who had done it, though Laura wasn't stupid. She knew that Delilah had gone into a private room with Pestilence and had come out with a bruised wrist. She also knew better than to press the issue. The Horsemen signed all their checks and all but owned their souls. Laura couldn't treat Pestilence like she could some customer who was out of line. *That* was the sole reason Delilah was still getting paid for the week off. Not her tips, of course, but her hourly rate.

She still hadn't wanted to see a doctor, hadn't wanted news of this incident to spread. The staff on the island might not break the veil of silence with outsiders, but they gossiped among themselves to a truly ridiculous degree. Delilah couldn't afford for the truth to get out.

Not when she had to keep her little sister safe.

Death stared at her for a long moment. "How long have you worked for us here on the island?"

"Two years." As if the woman had no idea. The Horsemen weren't people who left anything to chance, and that included their staff. To the best of Delilah's knowledge, they kept track not only of the people who actually worked for them, but also their families and close friends. It wasn't anything overt, but in her time working there, she'd heard more than a few offhand comments about debts being picked up and ultimatums being delivered. They allowed no influence but their own. No influence like the kind of threat currently leveled at Delilah's sister.

Death knows.

It took everything she had to keep her expression even under the other woman's stare. Death might be scarier than Delilah's father, but Delilah had learned to lie from birth.

Finally, Death nodded slowly. "I'll send the doctor." She turned for the door, but paused to glance over her shoulder. "When my brother comes around to apologize, try not to cower. It will make him feel guilty."

She cleared her throat. "I understand." No mistaking Death's priorities. If Pestilence was another man who'd hurt her, they would have made an example of him and then banished him from the island. Obviously, that wasn't an option with one of the four owners.

Her legs held her just long enough for the door to click behind Death. Then her knees morphed into jelly and Delilah sank to the floor. She'd just blown her only chance to get close to the Horsemen. Death had no interest in the club, Famine only came around when there were security issues and even then he only talked to Laura and the bouncers, not the dancers. War had spent the last few weeks occupied elsewhere, and that showed no sign of changing anytime soon.

Pestilence was her only option and she'd played her hand too soon.

Damn it, but she studied people as a matter of survival. She should have known that his tension wasn't desire. It was something significantly darker. No matter what Death thought, Pestilence wouldn't come around to apologize. Being a Horseman meant he held a near-godlike presence, and apologizing for *anything* would undermine that. Not to mention how scarily blank his expression had gone, as if he barely held himself back from doing worse.

Her gaze tracked to her bed, to the phone currently tucked under the mattress. She couldn't let Esther pay for her mistake. There had to be a way to fix this, and to do it fast. She just had to *think*. Maybe there was a way she could salvage this?

Another knock on her door had her heart leaping into her throat. Delilah hurried to answer, arranging her expression into one of peace. Her relief at seeing the doctor on retainer for the staff nearly had her toppling over. The only time this man came into the club was to help with small sprains and injuries the dancers suffered from time to time. He was a nice older guy with salt and pepper hair, dark brown skin, and kind eyes that always sought to put his patients at ease. He smiled. "Can I come in?"

Not one of the Horsemen at all. Just the promised medical attention. Since Death sent him, turning him away wasn't an option. She couldn't beg off by explaining she just suffered from a crippling case of bad impulse control. Delilah fought down her impatience and smiled. "Of course."

Twenty minutes later, she had a brace on her wrist and strict instructions not to do anything to strain it further for the next few days. Which meant no dancing … Which meant no tips. Not that either was an option with Laura sentencing her to rest and recover for the next seven days.

Alone again, she pressed her hands to her face. Maybe the answer wasn't on the island. Maybe leaving and flying back to New York to wade into Esther's mess in person was the better option. Her sister didn't make a habit of getting into big trouble—not like this—but there had been small shit that popped up from time to time as she went through high school. Little rebellions Delilah tried not to take too personally.

This was something else altogether. She couldn't write a check to beg Esther out of this trouble. Couldn't put on a sweet smile and charm her way through it. Couldn't do anything but dance on this high wire. One wrong step and both she and Esther would suffer.

As if summoned by her thoughts, the mattress buzzed beneath her.

They were calling again.

She rushed to the door to throw the deadbolt and then back to the bed to dig out the phone. Sure enough, the same number as before scrolled across the screen. It was too much to hope that they were calling to say this was all a horrible joke and everything was fine with Esther.

Delilah took a breath and then another. By the time she answered, she sounded calm and unruffled. "Hello?"

The man on the other end tsked. "Delilah, Delilah, Delilah. I never pegged you for someone who'd make such a marked misstep."

They knew. "What are you talking about?"

"We told you to get information on the Horsemen. Not to get mauled by one of them."

Cold rushed through her, the kind of fear she'd lived with day in and day out for eighteen long years. She looked at the fresh brace on her wrist. Barely two hours had passed since Pestilence grabbed her. It happened in a private room, and she'd only seen a handful of people between then and now. And somehow these people knew already.

The facts lined up in a nice little row, leading her to the only conclusion possible. They had others on the island. People reporting in on her and the Horsemen's movements.

She sank onto the bed. "I'm trying to do what you asked."

"You're fucking up." He sounded almost sympathetic, which was so much worse than any screaming threat. "It's really unfortunate. Your sister seems like a nice kid. It's a shame what's going to happen to her because you can't hold up your end of the bargain."

"Wait!" Delilah took a short breath and modulated her tone. "I'm doing the best I can."

"Come on, now. You know that's not good enough."

"Then have someone else on the island do it!"

Silence for a beat. Two. "You're the one we want, Delilah." His voice deepened, becoming coaxing and almost playful. "You're the exotic dancer who's caught the eye of someone important. It's like something out of a movie, a book, a fairytale. Once he gets a taste, he'll fall hopelessly in love with you. You've hooked him. Don't fuck it up in reeling him in."

Reeling him in?

She pinched the bridge of her nose. "You're talking in riddles. You said I fucked it up and now you're saying that I've hooked him? Which is it?"

He ignored her questions just like he had the last time he called. "Play it slow next time. We require access to his phone. You'll only need it long enough to send a text to this number and click a link we send you, then erase the evidence."

His phone.

She almost laughed. Might have if the situation wasn't so hopeless. "How am I supposed to do that?"

"You're a smart girl. You have to be in order to have come so far. I'm sure you'll figure it out. You have a week."

"A *week*? That's not enough time."

"Delilah." He sighed like she'd disappointed him. "You're really going to make me say it, aren't you?"

Her throat tried to close. "Say what?"

"If you don't get us access to his phone, we'll start in on your baby sister. One piece at a time. I'll be sure to record it so you don't miss a single one of her screams." He sounded bored while he recited the horrific threats. "It'd be a shame if you got her out of that church only to lose her like this, don't you think? You're a better sister than that."

Of course he knew about the *church*. Church. More like a compound.

No, she couldn't think about that now, couldn't afford to

be distracted. Esther's safety depended on it. She swallowed hard. "I'll do it."

"Good girl. That's what I thought you'd say." He hung up.

It took every bit of control Delilah had not to throw the cursed phone against the wall. How was she supposed to get access to Pestilence's phone when simply touching his chest was enough to incite that kind of violent response? She wasn't some amazing thief who could pick someone's pocket without them realizing it. All her skills lay in dancing—and surviving the shit the universe saw fit to throw at her.

She'd survive this, too. Both her and Esther would.

She looked at her door. If Death was right and Pestilence would come around to apologize … Leverage. His theoretical apology was nothing but leverage. She'd use it just like she used people's lusts against them to get the jobs she wanted, to make more tips, to smooth out the jagged edges of life. A double-edged sword, but Delilah cut more often than she was cut. She couldn't ask for more.

She'd find a way to keep Pestilence close, to keep him coming back around, and then she'd figure out how to deal with his phone. Without getting caught.

The Island of Ys might deal in sin, but there was truly only one unforgivable offense—disloyalty. If she went through with this, getting fired was the best possible outcome.

In reality, she was a whole lot more likely to get dead.

CHAPTER 3

*A*fter how things played out during the private dance, the last place Ryu should be was standing outside the door to Delilah's room. Coming here was inappropriate and, more, it would likely scare her to have him showing up like this after he fucking *assaulted* her. He ran his fingers through his hair, hating the way the truth tore through him like acid.

This was a mistake.

One in a long line of mistakes that centered around Delilah Velásquez.

He turned to leave just as the door opened, and then there she was, the woman whose presence tormented him even as she brought him peace. She had her hair pulled back, and her face was clear of makeup. That combined with her hoodie and tiny sleep shorts made her look younger, more like a co-ed at some university than the temptress who stalked the stage night after night.

His gaze fell to the brace around her wrist and his stomach went hollow. He'd done that to her. His lack of control had caused her pain, his demons too strong to deny even now. "I'm sorry." The words came out hoarse, as if he hadn't spoken in years.

She flinched, and he realized that he sounded furious instead of apologetic. "It's fine."

"It's not."

Delilah nibbled at her full bottom lip. "Do you want to come in?" She wouldn't quite meet his gaze. "No touching, I promise."

The attempt at humor only made him feel worse. Going into her room was the wrong call. He'd come to apologize, and apologize he had, even if he'd thrown the words at her like a weapon instead of offering them in good faith. Ryu hated the fear that came off her in waves, but he recognized it for the blessing it was. If Delilah was scared of him, she'd stay the fuck away from him and escape being tainted by all his bullshit.

"I ... Okay." What the fuck was he doing? He should be going to hunt down Kenzie so they could go a couple rounds in the ring, could spar until his head stopped spinning on his shoulders.

He sure as hell should *not* be following Delilah into her room, letting the door swing shut behind him, drinking in the sight of the one place on the island where she'd been allowed to make her mark. To make her home.

All the staff were housed in quarters tucked near the back of Pleasure, away from the main floor, and all the rooms were more or less identical. He didn't make a habit of visiting any of them or the people they housed, but Delilah had undeniably put her stamp on this space. The kitchen was sparkling clean with flowers in a vase near the window, a hammock hung from the porch out the sliding glass door, and there was a pile of what appeared to be her various costumes from her routines on her bed as if she'd been in the middle of laundry. It was all so ... normal.

"Drink?" Delilah wandered into the kitchen.

"No."

Her step hitched, but she covered it up with a quick smile that didn't quite meet her dark eyes. "I hope you don't mind if I have one."

He made her nervous. He *scared* her, and why not? He was Pestilence, and his reputation preceded him everywhere on this island. More than that, he'd already proven that he was dangerous to her specifically, apology or not. Ryu fought not to clench his fists, knowing damn well that she'd read it as a threat instead of outward manifestation of his frustration at himself. Finally, he said, "A drink would be nice."

She veered to the little cabinet next to the fridge and bent to pull it open. He tried not to ogle her ass in those tiny shorts—he really did—but the thin fabric rode up, baring the lower curves, and he had to fight back a curse. How could she be even sexier in these lounge clothes than she was in next to nothing? It didn't make any fucking sense.

Delilah pulled out a bottle of tequila with her injured hand and winced. "That's going to take some getting used to."

Ryu moved before he could think better of it. He stepped into the kitchen and gently pulled the bottle out of her hand. "You're a lefty."

"Oh. Yeah." She took a small step back. "How'd you know?"

"You're hurt and you're still reaching for stuff with that hand instinctively." It was only then that he realized exactly how close they were. Not touching—Ryu would have noticed *that*—but a few scant inches separated them. Something was off, though … He frowned down at her. "You're short."

Delilah blinked. "I'm exactly the right height."

Hell. He couldn't seem to help fucking up whenever it came to this woman. He watched her careful retreat and kicked himself for sounding so accusing. She *was* short, but then he'd never seen her without the sky-high heels on. In this moment, she was so incredibly human. So normal. It should have lessened the siren's pull she had on him.

But standing here in her kitchen, he couldn't stop himself from noticing how her hair smelled like coconut and that she'd painted her toenails a bright teal color. That she worried her bottom lip when she didn't know what to say. Tiny details that drew him in despite himself.

Everything about this woman drew him in despite himself.

She reached for the bottle, but he moved it out of her reach. "Sit."

There it was, a flash of temper in those dark eyes. So vastly preferred to her fear. "You're in *my* home."

"In the strictest sense of the definition, the entire Island of Ys is *my* home, which means I have precedent."

She opened her mouth, and seemed to remember who she was talking to. Ryu hated the way she wilted a little and gave a shaky nod. "Glasses are in the corner cabinet." She shifted back one step and then another, and then moved around the kitchen peninsula to sit on one of the barstools.

She was afraid of him.

Ryu could kick himself for being an idiot. Even without the Horsemen factor, he was a man who'd hurt her and then showed up at her home and started bossing her around. She had absolutely no assurance that he wouldn't hurt her again, and so she attempted to handle him. It might have pissed him off if the whole situation didn't make him feel so fucking sick. He didn't hurt people. Well, he didn't hurt people who didn't deserve it.

He pulled down two glasses and splashed a healthy dose of tequila into each. It wasn't his drink of choice, but it'd do in a pinch. He slid one glass to her. "You have no reason to believe this, but I truly am sorry. It won't happen again."

"I shouldn't have touched you." She reached for the glass

with her injured hand and seemed to remember herself at last moment. "It's against the rules."

And the Horsemen were known for punishing those who broke the rules on the island. Ryu clenched his jaw to keep his curses inside. They wouldn't do anything but undermine the point he was trying to prove. It might be better to let her believe that it *was* punishment. Anything else required an explanation, and explaining themselves to outsiders went against everything he and his siblings had done to create their reputations. "I—"

She blinked those big dark eyes at him. "Did you know my father is a preacher?"

The sheer suddenness of the subject change rocked him back on his heels. "No," he said slowly.

He'd done thorough background checks on Delilah and the only other person she had active connection with: her little sister, Esther. He knew they were born in Texas, knew that Delilah had acted as Esther's guardian since she was eighteen. There'd been no evidence of family in the last eight years, so he hadn't bothered to go back further. Not for an exotic dancer who didn't need particularly high clearance within the island's operations.

"Well, he says preacher. Really, it's got more of a cult feel." She spoke in a sort of rambling tone as if telling a vaguely boring story, as if Ryu wasn't holding his breath as he soaked up this new information about her. "Daddy had strong opinions about women—especially pretty women. Liked to beat the shit out of me in the name of religion when the mood hit him or he needed to make an example." She held up a hand. "This isn't a call for sympathy or anything. I'm just saying … I've seen some really bad stuff, and what happened in the private room doesn't even make the top twenty. It's fine. We're good. Absolutely no reason to dig into it."

He had absolutely no right to feel a bond over their

shared trauma, especially since he had no intention of telling her the sordid details of what he'd gone through as a child. Instead, he said, "You survived him, and now you dance."

"Now I dance." She smiled, a satisfied curling of her lips that sent a bolt of heat right through him. "It started off as sheer survival with a little rebellion thrown in. I escaped him when I was eighteen, and I was sorely unqualified to do most things. But I was always good at dancing."

Did she realize the gift she gave him with this truth? Sharing the past so freely, sharing her *pain* so freely …

It wasn't done. He barely knew how to handle it. Ryu leaned back against the counter. "You're one of the best."

"Yes. I am." She toyed with her mostly empty glass as if weighing her words. "You've watched me every night for the last few weeks. You came into the club periodically before then, but it's been nightly lately."

There wasn't a question in there. She seemed to do that a lot when she was nervous, speaking in leading sentences that didn't quite cross the line into actual query. Ryu took his tequila as a shot, closing his eyes as it burned its way down his throat. "I like watching." He meant to say, *I like watching you dance*, but somewhere along the way, the truth slipped free.

He couldn't even blame it on the alcohol. It was purely Delilah. Something about her blurred his edges in a way he couldn't get enough of. He thought it was the dancing, but even standing here in her presence was accomplishing the same thing.

He didn't want to leave.

He opened his eyes and spoke before he could think better of it. "Will you let me make this up to you?"

"There's nothing to make up." She gave him a surprisingly sweet smile. Like all the others, it didn't quite warm her eyes. "It's forgiven."

Clearly, it wasn't or she wouldn't be lying to him right now. Ryu had no right to demand her forgiveness, but … maybe he could earn it. He set his glass in her sink. "All the same, I'd feel better if you'd let me make amends."

She hesitated, clearly torn. For someone who essentially acted for a living, Delilah was shit at concealing her expressions. Every thought was written across her face, there for anyone who bothered to look. It was … refreshing. Finally, she nodded. "If that's what you want, Pestilence."

Pestilence.

Another reminder of his past, of the distance between them that neither could ever really cross. "Ryu. My name is Ryu." Now it was his turn to hesitate. "Don't use it in public, though."

"I won't." Another of those lying sweet smiles. "I promise."

He nodded, doing his damnedest not to think too hard about what his siblings would say about this turn of events. "I'll see you tomorrow."

"What's tomorrow?"

"Tomorrow I start making it up to you." The words came out like a snapped command instead of a request, but he didn't know how to shift them. It was too late, anyways. What was it about this woman that made him stick his foot in his mouth again and again? He didn't know. Spending more time with her could only be considered a mistake, but Ryu didn't give a fuck. He walked out her door and closed it softly behind him before he headed slowly back to the hub.

When they bought the island and started construction on the two casinos, Pleasure and Pain, they decided early on that Pleasure would be their main hub of operations. The rooms and halls had been built in an intentional warren, hiding passageways for staff to move about unseen. And even more passageways for the Horsemen alone. In the center of the building was *their* hub. The place where they lived and worked without having to worry about dealing with anyone but each other. Of the four of them, Ryu spent most time there. Under normal circumstances, he preferred dealing with computers to dealing with people.

Until now.

He half expected to find Amarante ready to pounce the second he walked through the door, but she wasn't the one waiting for him. No, it was Kenzie standing in front of the wall of monitors showing the various parts of Pleasure. Her mass of blond hair was pulled back from her face and she wore gym clothes—shorts and a sports bra. There were bruises lining her hips in the shape of fingerprints and he tried his damnedest not to think about his sister fucking her new … whatever Liam was. Boyfriend seemed so pedestrian, especially when the man had all but staked his claim on Kenzie the second he arrived on the island.

Especially when Liam had thrown his lot in with the Horsemen so fully.

Ryu didn't need to look closer to know Kenzie studied the camera angled on the hallway where Delilah's room was located. She turned and propped her hands on her hips. "You break one of our dancers, and I'm the last to know about it?"

"I didn't break her." He also didn't want to think too hard about the brace on her wrist and the fact that he was the reason behind it. Ryu didn't lose control. It was the very definition of who he was. He handled himself in any situation that arose and, if there any question about things spiraling beyond his reach, he avoided the situation. In fifteen years since they escaped their version of hell on earth, he'd never hurt someone—not unless he planned on it.

He'd also never let anyone get close to him the way Delilah did when she danced. He hadn't wanted to.

Kenzie frowned up at him, her hazel eyes concerned. "I figured you'd need some ring time."

29

A few rounds with his sister in the ring might just be enough to burn off the worst of the feeling churning in his gut. Easier to focus on the harm he'd delivered to Delilah than on the bigger issue at hand.

The father who sold him to Camp Bueller, along with more children than Ryu could handle thinking about. Not just him and Amarante, his own flesh and blood, but hundreds of others. Including Luca and Kenzie.

Ryu looked at his desk, at the trio of monitors set up there for his work. He had all the evidence anyone could ever need to prove that Fai Zhao was the man behind the curtain. Their very own bogeyman, and he'd been closer than any of them could have dreamed.

Kenzie sighed. "Yeah, thought so. Get changed and let's go."

For once, he didn't argue. Time and time again, Ryu had been the one offering the support Kenzie needed when the past rode her too hard. Violence was a part of his life, but he didn't crave it the same way she did.

Until now.

Thirty minutes later, they met in the boxing ring. Kenzie bounced a little. "You going to tell me about this woman?"

"No." He jabbed, testing her.

She danced easily out of the way. "I'm really hurt that I had to hear about her from *Luca*. He's barely out of the hospital bed and he's already got better gossip than I do. It's ridiculous." Kenzie kicked him in the thigh hard enough to stagger him.

"It's no one's business." He didn't really believe that, though. Anything that went down on the island was Horsemen business. More than that, anything that went down with the *Horsemen* was family business. And family business never stayed buried for long.

"Really? Because you had a whole hell of a lot to say about Liam a month ago."

"It's different." He faked a right hook and knocked her back with his left hand. "I'm not being chased down by an Irish mobster intent on— …" He caught Kenzie's ankle as she tried to kick him in the balls. "Low blow."

She laughed, the sound loud and bright and full of joy. Even in the darkest times, Kenzie always managed to bring a thread of light. It was a truth he enjoyed usually.

Not today.

A lot of things that used to be true no longer held up with the current reality bearing down on him. Ryu stepped back and dropped his hands. "My father is responsible."

Instantly, all amusement fled Kenzie's face. She didn't approach him, didn't reach out for him. She simply nodded. "Yeah, he is. I'm sorry."

"I should be apologizing to you. He's the one who put you in that place."

She shrugged. "He wasn't the only one responsible. Even if he was, *you* had nothing to do with it. So put down the cross, Ryu. It's not yours to bear."

"You don't understand."

She used his distraction against him and swept a kick that knocked him on his ass. Kenzie propped her hands on her hips and glared. "Don't do that."

"Don't do what?" He sat up. "Don't speak the truth?"

"Don't start separating us. That guy might have been your sperm donor, but *we* are your family." She offered her hand. "Amarante is right. You're downright maudlin right now. It's not a good look, Ryu."

"I am *not* maudlin." Kenzie always brushed off the ugly parts of life—or at least appeared to. She had faced down one of the worst perpetrators of her nightmares just a few weeks ago and, for all intents and purposes, she'd bounced back almost immediately. He envied her that. Ryu didn't bounce. It wasn't in his nature. "I don't know how to make this right."

"We make it right the same way we were always going to." She wiggled her hand until he took it and allowed her to pull him to his feet. Kenzie gave him a sunny smile. "We kill them all."

CHAPTER 4

*I*n the eight years since Delilah took Esther and stole away in her old beat-up truck, she had only called out of work a handful of times. When there was no guarantee of the next meal, when her *sister* depended on her, she couldn't afford to do stupid shit like get drunk and be too hungover to work. Ditto with sickness and injury.

She didn't drink during her work week. She always got her flu shot and took extra precautions to avoid sick people. She took particularly good care of her body in an effort to keep from getting injured doing something stupid.

Look at her now.

She glared at the brace around her wrist. Even though it was only bruised, It definitely looked worse than it was, which should have been a relief, except she still had to wait for the bruises to fade before she could go back to work. A week should be enough. It *had* to be enough time for everything to get back to normal.

She didn't have to worry about money quite as intensely as she had at eighteen, but Esther was probably going to be a surgeon someday, and at roughly fifty-five grand a year, the rest of her college amounted to a whole lot of money for Delilah to come up with. Two years into Esther's degree and she had the rest of the money for her undergraduate degree saved up. Spending a few years being hungry and desperate and not sure when their next meal would show up was enough to give her a hoarder mentality when it came to finances. All it took was one bad turn and she'd be back there again.

One bad turn and *Esther* would be back there again.

Dark thoughts led her to the phone. *Her* phone, not the one tucked back in its safe place under her mattress. She did a quick calculation of the time difference and called Esther.

Surely she was still safe. They gave Delilah a week. No reason to think they'd do something before then. But considering she didn't know who *they* were, she wasn't about to put anything up to chance. She held her breath as the phone rang and rang. Finally, it clicked over and a sleepy, "Do you even know what time it is?" filled the line.

Delilah exhaled in relief. "Sorry, sis. I thought for sure you'd be up. Don't you have a big test in a couple days?"

"Yes." Rustling as Esther must have rolled over. "But I'm not an idiot. I've spent a ton of time studying. I know the material backward and forward."

Her throat burned and she had to blink rapidly. "That's my girl." Her baby sister was destined for greatness. She was too smart and too ambitious for anything resembling a normal life, an intelligence and personality that had been the bane of Delilah's existence when she was twelve. Now, at twenty? The sky was the limit.

She would do absolutely anything to ensure that *nothing* limited Esther's climb to her dreams.

Silence for a beat, and when her sister spoke again, she sounded less sleepy. "Is everything okay? You're usually working this time, aren't you?"

"Uh, yeah." Crap. Delilah should have realized she would question her calling like this. They always talked Sunday afternoons, Esther's time. Calls off that schedule usually meant voicemail because Esther was in class or Delilah was on the stage. "There was a small accident—nothing serious— but I sprained my wrist. I'm out for a week."

"Are you okay?"

Not even close, but it had nothing to do with the throbbing of her wrist and everything to do with her worry about the next seven days. "You know me, sis. I'm always okay."

Esther sighed. "I'm not a kid anymore, Delilah. You don't have to keep putting on a brave face for me. If I need to get a job—"

She burst out laughing. "Honey, I have your entire undergraduate covered and another chunk of change set aside for expenses. Worry about school. I have the money covered."

This time, her silence lasted longer. "Is it Dad?"

"*No.*" Eight years, and they still looked over their shoulders for the man who'd spent so many years making their lives a living hell. Such was the power of their father, that he could reach across time and space and still keep them up at night. Delilah had to take a breath and force the tension from her voice. "I'm still keeping track of him. He's in Texas." He'd started a new church down there and was preaching along his favorite topic—the rapture. He'd be occupied with that for ages yet, but that wouldn't stop me from checking up on him weekly.

"It's a pretty quick flight from Texas up here."

"He doesn't know where we are. As far as he's concerned, we're dead." It's what he told all his parishioners about a year after they escaped. He'd even held a funeral for them with empty coffins—and live-streamed it on social media. Watching those coffins go into the ground was one of the more surreal experiences of Delilah's life. "You're safe,

Esther." A lie, that. If her sister was safe, Delilah wouldn't be endlessly pacing her room, wondering how the hell she was going to pull off the task set in front of her.

Betray the Horsemen.

Betray Pestilence.

No, not Pestilence.

Ryu.

She pressed a hand to her chest, hating the strange feeling hearing his actual name brought. He shared it in a trust she didn't deserve—one she'd already set out to betray. Yes, he hurt her. Yes, he scared the shit out of her. But Delilah would suffer through a lot worse to keep this job. Without the last two years on the Island of Ys, she wouldn't be able to pay for her sister's college. Not so quickly, at least. Another couple months and she'd have be able to start in on the fund for Esther's graduate degree.

"Delilah?" From the way her sister said her name, it wasn't the first time.

"It's fine. We're fine." She forced an easy smile into her voice. "Tell me what's new with you."

"We just talked a few days ago."

"You haven't done *anything* interesting in those few days? What about that girl you're interested in? Did you finally get the nerve to ask her out?"

Esther huffed out a laugh. "Not all of us are as ballsy as you are, big sister. I don't know if she's flirting with me or just being nice."

"Only one way to find out."

"Easy for you to say. You're like a ten and have ass for days."

A conversation they'd had more times than Delilah could count. "It's all about confidence, Esther. Just fake it until you make it."

Her sister groaned. "Fine, I'll ask her out for coffee."

"Worst she can say is no."

"Are you really trying to comfort me with worst case scenarios right now? This is not how pep talks are supposed to work."

Delilah laughed. "Good luck, though you don't need it. Not for the girl and not for the test."

"I'm not worried about the test."

Esther sounded so grumpy that some of her worry melted away. She'd find a way through this. She'd carried them through worse situations over the years, though Delilah was hard pressed to think of one that came close. It didn't matter. Her priorities came down to Esther and only Esther. "I love you, kid."

"I love you, too."

"I'll call Sunday at the usual time." Hopefully, she'd have everything handled by then. Five days. Not very long in the grand scheme of things, but Delilah was uniquely motivated.

"Cool." Esther yawned. "Talk to you then."

She hung up and dropped her phone onto her bed. Pestilence—Ryu—said he'd make it up to her, but she couldn't afford to sit around and wait for him to follow through on his word. If he even intended to do it. The Horsemen were usually good for their promises, but Delilah only had experience with the business aspect of it. This might have started out that way, but it had veered personal pretty damn quickly.

She really shouldn't have touched him.

She sat on the bed. "Okay, honesty time." She could pretend she was just trying to follow through on the fantasy the private rooms provided. They weren't supposed to touch the customers, but a little lap dance only smudged the line a little. Delilah usually didn't cross that line, but every once and awhile the money was good enough to tempt her.

Ryu hadn't offered her money.

He hadn't even offered her words.

He just stared at her with those bottomless dark eyes that held so much need and desire, Delilah's instincts had over-ridden her good sense. He was magnet to her lodestone. Or lodestone to her magnet. However that metaphor went. Before he started coming to the club regularly, she hadn't believed in the kind of chemistry that could reach across a crowded room and slap her in the face. But she always, *always*, knew when he was in the audience when she danced. And when they were alone?

She shivered.

Yeah, she hadn't touched him to provide his fantasy. She'd done it because she lost control and forgot herself. The very thing she couldn't afford to do on the island in general—and in particular during the next five days. Touching Ryu was completely off limits. Thinking of him as anything other than a mark was even more off limits.

She sighed. If only she could turn off her emotions as easily as she turned on the charm and seduction routine. The Horsemen were … larger than life. And they squashed their enemies without second thought. She'd heard rumors of what they did to people who crossed them, who broke the rules. When Ryu went after them, there usually was a person left behind to regret their mistakes. But when Death or War were the ones delivering punishment? People *disappeared*, and not just from the internet. Was it really outside the realm of possibility that they'd done something to deserve this?

Except I've never heard of the Horsemen threatening innocents to get the job done.

Delilah put it from her mind. At the end of the day, it didn't matter. They were her employers, yes, but Esther was her sister. Family trumped everything else.

With that in mind, she dressed carefully. Cut-off shorts with more holes than fabric and a cropped lacy tank top that left her stomach bare. She let her hair hanging in loose waves around her shoulders and only applied a little tinted gloss to her lips. Leather sandals on her feet and the image was complete. Sexy as hell, but in a casual sort of way that looked like she wasn't trying too hard.

She took a deep breath and stared at herself in the mirror. "You can do this. You've spent your whole damn life selling the lie on stage. The world's just another kind of stage." Her little pep talk didn't make her feel better, but she wasn't sure anything could make her feel better at this point.

Delilah didn't let herself hesitate further. She marched out the door and into the hallway. It was only as she headed for the main casino floor that she realized she didn't have anything resembling a plan. Oh well. She'd already jumped. Figuring things out on the way down was what she did.

She didn't have a choice.

A few minutes of wandering had her about ready to go out of her skin. Before shit hit the fan, Delilah worked six days a week. She *liked* working. But it meant she didn't usually choose to partake in any of the entertainments the Island of Ys had to offer.

With that in mind, she turned to the entrance and headed out of the aggressively air-conditioned building. The heat slapped her in the face and Delilah grinned despite herself. She didn't usually miss Texas, but living for years in New York was enough to have her longing for the milder winters. Coming to the island to work would have been a blessing if she spent more time outside.

She headed down the pretty paved walkway that led to the beach. The Island of Ys was actually three islands, though only one of them held all the entertainment. It was shaped a little like a crab with its pinchers nearly touching. On the north side was Pleasure. The south housed Pain.

Delilah stopped to untie her sandals and slip them off her feet. She usually avoided Pain and the darker pleasures it offered: fucking, both vanilla and specialized kink; high stakes card games where more money was exchanged than she'd see in her lifetime; the monthly fights in the ring.

A woman could get into a lot of trouble in that place if she wasn't careful. Delilah had been here long enough to see it happen. Girls who got their heads messed up by the rich men and women who patronized the island, who believed lies spun in order to get access to what the patrons wanted— their bodies. Eventually the patrons always left, and they never took their island flings with them.

She had no time for that, no interest in getting entangled. Even if she was willing to have a fling, no one had pulled at her interest enough to outweigh all the other baggage Delilah carried around. Impossible to let herself get swept away when she was all too aware of the cost.

Her current and future security.

Esther's future.

The very things on the line right now.

She released a pent-up breath and started walking. The beach spread parallel to the boardwalk that stretched between Pleasure and Pain, populated with a variety of little shops and tiny bars for the people who wanted a more "authentic" island experience. She snorted. As if there was anything authentic about the Island of Ys. It was all carefully curated to meet and exceed expectations.

She stopped halfway down the beach and sank onto one of the lounge chairs. If she concentrated, she could almost pretend she was well and truly alone, that nothing the world could bring to bear was enough to send her to her knees. That the danger had long since passed.

Delilah felt him even before she turned to see Ryu striding down the sand toward her. The invisible connection between them thrummed and her body went tight. It was easier to ignore her reaction on stage. She had half a dozen things to keep track of—her dance and pole routine, her expression, her slow stripping seduction—and an inconvenient attraction only heightened the performance.

You're in the middle of a performance right now.

Right. Something she couldn't afford to forget.

She lifted her hand to shield her eyes so she could watch Ryu cross the last bit of distance. He wore a tailored suit, the heat pressing against her skin apparently unable to touch him. The barest sheen of sweat on his forehead gave lie to the illusion, and she liked him better for being human enough to sweat. He scowled fiercely enough, it was a wonder the very elements didn't shrink back from him.

She should be shrinking back from him. This man was *dangerous*. Dangerous in general, and dangerous to her specifically. If he found out the truth of why she'd agreed to spend more time in proximity with him ... The very best-case scenario involved her losing her bank account and all the data that proved she existed. Even if he didn't kill her, she'd be worse off than she was at eighteen. Delilah didn't know how to get a new social security card, let alone how she was supposed to get back into the U.S. without a passport. Obviously, it could be done, but she didn't have the skills or knowledge to pull it off.

Even with all those fears circling her mind like vultures, Delilah couldn't help but acknowledge what an attractive scene he created as he stalked toward her. Ryu wasn't quite as tall as Famine—maybe six foot, give or take—and he was built leaner through the shoulders, too. More rapier than broadsword. In the end, it didn't matter because the person on the other side of the blade still ended up bleeding out.

He moved with a lethal grace she couldn't help but appreciate. Rumor had it that he and War sparred in the fighting ring from time to time and, if one was lucky enough to catch a few seconds of it, it was a sight to behold. Delilah believed it. Ryu moved like he knew death.

But then, Death was his sister, so that made sense.

An absurd laugh bubbled up in her throat, and it was everything she could do to keep it internal. Instead, Delilah propped her hands back on the lounge chair behind her and waited. The position arched her back and pressed her breasts against the tight lace of her top, and if he looked closely, he'd be able to see the faint outline of her nipples. He wanted her. He wouldn't watch her so closely while she danced if he didn't. It was up to her to use that attraction to stay one step ahead of him.

Ryu slowed. "Delilah."

This probably counted as being in public, so instead of debating which name to use, she simply worked up a smile. "Hey."

"How's your arm feeling?"

In truth, it ached something fierce currently and she shouldn't be putting even this much pressure on it, but she wouldn't hold his attention with pity and guilt. The Horsemen had none of either. No, Delilah's only hope lay in being *interesting*. "I'd really rather not talk about my arm right now."

Ryu gracefully sank onto the next lounge chair over. "I *am* sorry." He didn't quite lob the words at her the way he had yesterday, but they still sounded like they'd been forcefully yanked from his throat.

"You already said that." She leaned back and stretched her legs out. Even behind his sunglasses, she could feel his eyes on her. Even as she told herself it was the very height of insanity, her body went a little hot under his gaze. "Like I said yesterday, you have nothing to apologize for."

"That brace on your wrist says otherwise."

Hard to argue that, but this was Pestilence. One of the

Four Horsemen. If there was anywhere that he could do what he wanted without consequences, it was on the Island of Ys. That kind of power would go to a normal person's head, would corrupt them until they were a shadow version of themselves. Look at her father; he gained a handful of followers in his little church and became a tyrant.

She didn't know why Pestilence insisted on apologizing to her. Maybe Death made him do it. He seemed sincere enough, but she'd grown up with one of the most accomplished liars Delilah had ever known. She'd seen how easily it was to use words and body language to make people believe anything a person wanted.

His mouth twisted. It was a nice mouth, wide and expressive though it seemed more inclined to frown than smile. Pestilence leaned forward and propped his elbows on his knees. "I would like to make things right."

Yeah, right. It was much more likely that he had ulterior motives, just like she did. The only difference is that she didn't think *hers* would end up with Delilah or Esther disappearing. She tilted her sunglasses down and looked at him over the rims. How to play this?

Be interesting. Sure. Easier to be interesting when she was dancing and lust short-circuited people's brains. Conversation was infinitely more complicated. "Pestilence, you own this island. Or at least one fourth of it. The Island of Ys isn't attached to any particular country and the only laws here are the ones the Horsemen put into place. If you wanted to slaughter your way through the guests staying here, there isn't a single person who could or would stop you."

"You have a point."

Impossible to miss the way he didn't jump in and say that slaughtering people was something he'd never do. Delilah fought down a shudder. "Yes, I have a point." She lifted her

43

wrist. "This is small potatoes. I broke the rules. You punished me for it. End of story."

Ryu studied her for a long moment, but his sunglasses shielded his thoughts from her. Finally, he turned to look out over the water. "Do you swim?"

Fear surged and she gripped the chair to keep from shaking. Surely he couldn't know that particular secret? As soon as the thought crossed her mind, she almost snorted. What was she saying? The Horsemen dealt in secrets as often as they dealt in violence. Despite her efforts, her voice came out strained. "Why would I swim?"

Ryu still didn't look at her, his attention on the water. "You live on an island. It seems like a waste if you don't swim."

Thank you very much for reminding me of the fact that I'm trapped here. She dug her toes into the sand, a physical reminder that a whole lot of land stood between her and the deep, blue sea. It wasn't like this island would share the fate of its legendary predecessor. A gate opened and the waters rushing in to drown everyone in the French version of Atlantis. Delilah shuddered again. Maybe she could brazen her way through this minefield of a conversation. "There are a lot of predators in the ocean. Though one could argue that there are even more predators on land."

He turned back to face her and the tension in his body sent alarm bells clanging through her head. "You can't swim."

A secret she'd carried with her for years and years and years. Even Esther didn't know that Delilah couldn't swim, because Delilah would have had to explain *why*. Her little sister carried enough trauma from her time in their father's home. She didn't need to carry Delilah's, too. In the past, she'd always covered it up with fancy swimsuits and full make-up and hair. Better to be believed to be too extra to get wet than the truth. That she was too afraid.

She swallowed hard. "What makes you think I can't swim?"

"I *know* you can't. What I don't know is why."

When she'd set out to be interesting, she hadn't anticipated having to bare parts of herself to a man who looked at her like she was an interesting bug under a microscope. Oh, he desired her, but most people did on one level or another. Those people didn't *study* her the way Ryu did.

She could beg off. He might scare the shit out of her, but she was reasonably sure he wouldn't pin her down and force her to expel her truths to him. At least not at this juncture. But running away wouldn't get her closer to his phone—to saving Esther. She could do this. All she had to do was tell the truth. One tiny, traumatizing truth.

"My father was—is—all Old Testament fire and brimstone. His greatest failure was having daughters instead of sons, and my being attractive was the greatest sin of all. Temptation and all that." She tried to casually wave that away, but her hand shook too much to really pull it off. "He tried a variety of ways to cure me of my sin. The methods don't matter much, but one of his favorites was baptism."

Ryu's stillness was entirely too predatory for her peace of mind. She couldn't tell if he was looking at her as prey or if he was thinking of ways he'd like to dismantle her father, piece by piece. Even his voice was curiously calm when he said, "I was under the impression that people are only required to be baptized once."

"He decided that mine didn't take." If she concentrated, she could still feel the imprint of her father's hands on her shoulders, shoving her beneath the water, could see the blurry outline of his face through the surface disturbed by the last of the oxygen leaving her lungs. Over and over again, blackness would take her, only to be replaced by an aching chest and the cool tile of the bathroom beneath her cheek.

Those moments of waking up were the only times Delilah's determination to survive actually stuttered and she wondered if it wouldn't be better to move to a place beyond, where he couldn't hurt her.

Only the knowledge that she'd leave Esther behind kept her climbing back to her feet, over and over again.

Ryu tilted his head to the side. "Would you like to learn?"

No. The very last thing she wanted to do was get into water, let alone get into water with a dangerous man. She didn't know why he was digging into this part of her past or what his motivation was for offering this thing she most definitely didn't want …, but Delilah had no choice. She couldn't afford to pass up any chance to get closer to him, no matter how her mind and body rebelled at the thought. Maybe they already knew about the phone and this was all some elaborate plan to kill her and stage it as an accident?

It didn't matter. She had *no choice*.

Delilah forced a smile. "Are you offering?"

"Yeah, I guess I am." He jerked his chin toward Pleasure. "Come on."

CHAPTER 5

*R*yu hadn't intended to end up in a pool with Delilah Velásquez, but his shock at hearing she couldn't swim overrode everything else. They were on an *island*, for fuck's sake. What if something happened and she drowned simply because she didn't have the skills necessary? Unthinkable.

And the reason behind it? He'd made a mental note to dig deep into her history and find out where this father of hers currently lived. The man deserved to be punished for what he'd put Delilah through—and Ryu suspected that the *baptisms* were only skimming the surface—and anyone who abused power like that with their own children wouldn't hesitate to do it to others under their power.

He might have laughed at the realization that they had *that* in common, if on different scales. It didn't lessen the horror of what she'd gone through, of course. Ryu wasn't all that inclined to offer up his own history to let her know she wasn't alone. Some things were better left to the dark to rot.

That said …, he wanted to give Delilah a better memory. A gift of sorts since there wasn't much she couldn't buy herself, and throwing money at a problem felt crass. This was something meaningful that he could do to balance out the harm he'd dealt her.

He hoped.

Ryu hadn't thought through the implications of his offer until the moment she appeared in a wrap that barely covered her curves. The first warning bell went off, increasing in volume as he led her to the private indoor pool designated for Horsemen use. It was really only Amarante who utilized the space, swimming laps until her plans fell into place in her head. She wouldn't be able to relax if it was available to the general public, so it was only family allowed in here, which meant the room usually lay empty.

Just like it was now.

Ryu had changed quickly after their conversation on the beach, and thankfully none of his siblings were around to question why he had dragged his mostly unused swimsuit out of a drawer. He felt particularly naked without his usual suit, and that feeling coupled with the woman who stood just out of reach, taking in the pool, left him in a bad way. "No one will bother us here."

"If you were anyone else, that might sound like you're making a pass at me." She moved away before he could think about that too hard—and fuck, he tried not to. Her next words were the equivalent of dumping cold water over his head. "Or that you're going to off me."

"I'm not going to *off* you." He also wasn't going to make a pass at her. Doing so was out of line for a thousand different ways. She worked for him, even if it wasn't directly. He'd *hurt* her, intentionally or not. And there was the small factor that he was about to do the equivalent of ride off into war with his own fucking father. No, spending more time with Delilah was selfish and wrong and a dick move.

She shrugged out of her wrap and Ryu forgot to breathe.

In the last forty-eight hours, he'd seen Delilah done up for the stage, he'd seen her barefoot and rumpled, and he'd seen her in what passed for beach wear. He'd *dream* about the way those shorts hugged her ass.

None of it compared to her in a tiny neon-green bikini.

She tugged at the tie on the bottoms, the first gesture he'd seen her make that betrayed her nerves. "When I bought this, I was thinking more about the lack of tan-lines than I was about actual functionality."

He barely, *barely*, kept a comment internal about how she wouldn't have shit for tan-lines with so little fabric to work with. She was obviously nervous and leering at her made him the worst kind of asshole. Ryu cleared his throat, his voice coming out in a rumble. "It's a swimsuit. It'll work."

Delilah turned to look at the pool and he choked. The back was a fucking *thong*. Her perfectly rounded ass spoke of plenty of time in the gym, and it was everything he could do not to drop to his knees and …

And what?

Touch her?

Press his mouth to her skin and see if she tasted as good as he imagined?

Ryu turned away and took several slow breaths. Delilah was *off limits*. If he couldn't keep that truth straight, he had no business spending any time with her, making up for his dick move or not. Falling on her like a starving man was a thousand times worse than what he'd done to her wrist.

"Ryu?"

His name on her lips almost undid him completely. He ran his hands over his face, fighting for control. "Yeah?"

"Is everything okay?" She still sounded nervous, like she might bolt if he made a sudden move.

He scrubbed his hands over his face, surprising himself by answering honestly. "I wasn't expecting the thong."

A thread of amusement worked its way into her warm tone. "Do you want me to go buy a different suit?"

Goddamn it, he could do better than this. He gave himself a full three seconds to regain control and finally turned back to her. "No. It's fine." It wasn't fine. It wasn't anywhere *near* fine. He'd get over it, though. They could stand there talking as his control slowly unraveled, piece by piece, or they could do what he'd brought her here to do. "Let's get this over with." He took two steps and dove into the water.

The coolness slapped some sense into him. If he could teach Delilah how to swim, that would be sufficient payment for the wrong he'd done. Oh, he'd already transferred monetary compensation into her employee account, but Ryu knew better than most that money didn't really fix anything. It helped. It helped a whole hell of a lot, but simply throwing a bunch of zeroes at Delilah after what he'd done was insult to the injury he caused.

He had to make it right.

Teaching her how to swim would make it right.

He surfaced to find her standing before the stairs into the water. Her white-knuckled grip on the railing matched the tension lining her body. She still hadn't taken that first step into the pool. "I really don't know if this is a good idea."

Ryu swam to the shallow end and stood. "I won't let anything happen to you." A statement he had no business making.

She reluctantly moved down to the first step and then the second. "Did I mention that this is a great way to make my death look like an accident? Because it is. If you're going to kill me, torturing me first is really rude."

"Delilah, I'm not going to kill you."

She shot him a look. "Consider me not comforted in the least." But she cautiously moved the rest of the way until the water lapped at her ribs. At her barely covered breasts.

Fuck. Stop ogling her.

He wanted to set her at ease, but it was never a skill Ryu cultivated. The only people he usually cared about were his siblings, and simply existing was enough to put them at ease. Everyone else? He'd never bothered. In fact, he'd worked hard to ensure the opposite reaction. These days, his reputation did most of the work for him on a day to day basis. People bent over backwards not to piss him off, and that made his life easier. It also meant Delilah was scared of him, of what he was capable of.

The thought made him sick to his stomach, but he'd spent too many years ensuring he emanated danger. He didn't know how to turn it off. Ryu wasn't even sure it was possible to turn it off when it'd melded so thoroughly to every part of him.

Still, he could try. He looked away and pulled forth a little honesty. "I didn't grab you in the private room because you broke the rules. I don't like being touched by strangers." Touched by people he didn't trust, people who could and would hurt him just like he'd been hurt as a child. Even offering this small bit of information had his gut churning. Some things, it was easier not to talk about, to shove the pain and fear into the past where it belonged.

He'd left that scared little boy behind when he left the camp. He was *strong* and scary and more than capable of taking care of both himself and the people around him. But no one could have survived what he did without scars, internal or otherwise. His brother Luca wore those scars on his body. The rest of them wore marks of their trauma in ways that weren't as easy to spot.

"I see," Delilah said slowly, seeming to turn that new piece of information over in her head. Finally, she frowned. "Uh, Ryu, I hate to be the one to bring this up, but how the hell are you going to teach me to swim without touching me?"

He really didn't want to keep talking about this. Bad enough to even mention it. Digging in was out of the question. "Don't worry about it."

"What happens if I start to drown? Are you just going to glare at me really hard until I float?" She took a step back, her breath coming too fast. "This was a mistake."

No two ways around it. He was fucking this up. He held up his hands. "Delilah, wait." The next words stuck in his throat, but he powered through. "The touching thing only goes one way. I can touch you without losing it." He couldn't promise safety. Not in life, and not on the island. Not anymore.

But he could promise her this. "I won't let you drown."

"Oh." Nothing in her tone to give away her thoughts. For once, nothing in her expression gave him any help, either. Delilah gave herself a little shake. "So what you're saying is that as long as I don't touch *you*, we're good." A slow smile pulled at her lips. "But *you* can touch *me*." Enough innuendo there to sink a ship.

He muscled down his body's reaction. She was just making jokes so she didn't feel afraid. She didn't mean anything by it. He couldn't afford to assume she meant anything by it. "That's what I'm saying."

"Huh." She laughed suddenly. "Okay, Ryu. Teach me how to swim."

He walked her through the motions required to tread water, and Delilah looked a little put-upon but followed his instructions exactly. She had a point. The best way to really learn was to get her deeper. He glanced at the other end of the pool. "Come on."

"You gave me a five-minute prep and you want me to just waltz into the deep end?"

"Yes."

Delilah took a slow breath and waded after him, the

water rising higher and higher until it reached her chin. She winced. "I changed my mind. This is a terrible idea. I know you said you want to make things up to me, but this feels a whole lot like punishment."

"It's not a punishment." He motioned for her to keep going. "A little farther."

She bit her bottom lip. "What happens if I go under?"

He hated that she was afraid. "Just move your arms like I showed you. Nice and smooth. Don't fight the water. Don't panic." He spoke slowly, calmly, trying to infuse her with something besides trepidation. She could do this. If she could pull off some of the gravity-defying moves on the pole that she managed with ease, she could tread water. She *had* to learn to tread water, even if she never swam.

"I'm already panicking."

"Delilah." He didn't mean to put so much snap into his voice, but he couldn't help it. "You live on an island. There are a dozen ways something could go bad in a way that ended with you in the water. If you can't at least tread water, you'll drown." When she still hesitated, he fought down the fear demanding he shake some sense into her. "It's a stupid fucking way to die when you have someone standing here offering to teach you."

"You are such an asshole," she breathed. She took a bracing breath and bobbed a little farther down the slope. So far, so good. Right up until the moment she stopped touching. Her eyes went wide and she went under for a moment. He held was already moving, but Delilah surfaced with a curse.

Good. She had it. She …

Except she didn't have it. Delilah wasn't doing the slow movements he'd taught her. She fought the water, the struggle taking her farther into the deep end. She thrashed, splashing him in the face.

By the time he blinked water from his eyes, she went under. "Fuck!"

Ryu lunged forward and grabbed her arms, hauling her up to the air. Delilah let loose a little screech. She was wrapped around him like a spider monkey, her legs around his waist, her arms around his torso, her head tucked down against his chest.

He froze, his body flashing hot and cold and hot again. Too much sensation, too much stimulation, too much. He held his arms away from his body, away from her, and forced himself to take in every detail of this, to hold it up as evidence that he wasn't back in that room.

Water. So much water. Salt and something briny in the air. Delilah wrapped around him, chanting "I'm sorry, I'm sorry, I'm sorry."

The pressure in his chest didn't dissipate, but he managed to clear his throat, to ground himself in the here and now to the point where he wasn't afraid he'd lose control again. He tentatively touched her hips. "I've got you."

"I'm sorry." She didn't loosen her grip in the least. "I can't let go yet."

Did she realize she'd clung to *him* as her safe space? No point in looking into that. He was simply a warm body, a stable piece in the midst of the pool to keep her safe. Ryu ran a hand down her back. "I've got you," he repeated. "You're safe."

"Safe." Delilah let out a surprisingly rough laugh. "I think we both know that's not the truth."

Yeah, he guessed they did. "Guess I should have brought you flowers to apologize instead.

"Flowers." Delilah lifted her head to meet his gaze. She still shook badly enough that he wanted to pull her closer, to hold her tightly until she knew she was safe. Except she *wasn't* safe. None of them were. She gave a sad smile. "Flowers are a sweet thought."

Sweet. He didn't think he'd ever been called that before. He sure as hell shouldn't be called it by this woman. "I'm not sweet."

"No. You're really not." She gave a little shrug and there went the lip bite again. Delilah shifted. "I guess we should go back to the shallow spot."

He immediately started walking them in that direction. As much as he was getting used to the feeling of Delilah in his arms, he wouldn't keep her stranded out there simply because he didn't want to let her go. There had to be lines. There fucking *had* to be.

The fact her swimsuit still covered any part of her after the thrashing was a small miracle, but each ragged breath had her breasts rubbing against his chest and the material shifting a little closer to exposing her nipples. He was a special kind of bastard to want to nudge it aside and see her. To memorize the sight of her in the light of the pool instead of the shadows of the club.

He stopped while they were still waist-deep in the water and studied the way she worked that bottom lip. "Do you want me to put you down?"

"I don't know." Delilah shifted again, and this time there was no way it was an accident. Not with her rolling her hips in a way that somehow managed to guide his hands to her ass. Or maybe that was all Ryu. He couldn't be sure. She shivered. "We really shouldn't."

"I know." But he found himself wading through the water to the edge of the pool anyways. "I'm your boss."

"Technically Laura is my boss."

"I'm Laura's boss."

They reached the edge and Delilah released him with her

55

arms, though she kept her legs locked around his waist. She leaned back and clamped her hands on the edge of the pool.

So she wouldn't touch him.

Ryu studied her face, trying to divine her thoughts. He wasn't the best at people reading—computers made far more sense to him—but he suspected Delilah would confound even the best. Had he really thought every expression played out across her face? Right now, he couldn't figure out what she wanted at all. "You're safe."

"I'm really not." Her breath hitched. "Touch me, Ryu. Before I realize what a crappy idea this is."

"You're not creating a compelling argument."

"Aren't I?" She didn't reach for him. No, she did something significantly more devastating. She pulled the ties of her top. A single tug and they were free. The wet fabric clung to her skin, and she peeled it off her and tossed the top away.

Baring herself to him.

He'd seen her breasts before. Time and time again while sitting in the audience or occupying the private room. This was different. This wasn't solely watching, not when he had her wrapped around him, not when every shallow breath she took made them rise and fall as if in invitation.

"I stand corrected." He kept one hand on her ass and pressed the other between her breasts, where he could feel her heart racing against his palm. She looked like some kind of goddess who'd deigned to grant him a favor, her dark hair falling in wet tangles around her shoulders, droplets of water dripping across her skin, her brown nipples pebbled and goosebumps rising on her skin.

He could lift her up and suck one and then the other into his mouth. He could set her on the edge of the pool and draw her swimsuit bottoms off. He could ...

Except he couldn't.

Ryu had little in the way of honor, but there were some

lines that couldn't be crossed. Not with the Horsemen's people. *Especially* not with this one.

"This isn't what I brought you down here for." Another moment and he'd have himself wrestled back under control. He'd stop thinking about how easy it would be to escalate things, instead of making the right choice.

Just one more moment.

"Ryu," she breathed his name as if she was just as conflicted as he was. "You're right. We shouldn't, ..." Delilah arched into his touch. "But I really, really want to."

He had to stop this.

He *had* to.

"Delilah," he murmured. "This wasn't part of the plan."

"It wasn't part of my plan, either."

Maybe another time, he'd wonder what her plan was. What aspirations she had for the future. How she'd come from a troubled history to end up on the Island. If she was anyone else, if they were in any other position, he would be wondering at it right now. It's what Ryu did. He tugged at strings of information and followed them back to their inevitable conclusions.

This moment felt like a different kind of inevitable conclusion.

Ryu ran a single finger down the curve of her breast to circle her nipple. He closed his eyes, but it only made the sensation of so much of her pressed against so much of him more acute. Not her hands. She made sure of that. But she was an inferno in the midst of all this water.

He wanted to burn. Just this once. "Let me make you feel good, Delilah."

She shivered. "You have no idea how sexy it is when you say my name like that."

"Like what?"

"All rumbly, like you're thinking about doing half a dozen

truly filthy things to me and you can't figure out which one to start with."

He leaned down until each inhale had their chests brushing. "I'm thinking I want your taste on my tongue." God, he wanted it more than he wanted his next breath. This was even better than watching her dance. Touching her shorted out something in his brain, leaving his racing thoughts blessedly blank in a way Ryu wasn't ready to give up. Not yet.

She gave a hoarse laugh. "Then by all means, Ryu … Taste me."

He immediately moved back enough to turn her around to face the edge of the pool. There were mirrors lining every other wall panel on this side of the room. With one arm banded across her waist, he lifted her high enough that they could both see her breasts but not her hips.

And him?

He looked completely out of control.

"Hands on the ledge. Don't move them."

"Okay." She smiled a little in the mirror at him. "You really do like to watch, don't you?"

"Yes." A couple of tugs and the bottoms of her swim suit were gone. He had Delilah Velásquez naked in his arms, and he hadn't done a single damn thing to deserve the privilege. He spread his hand over her stomach and met her gaze in the mirror. "Are you sure, Delilah?"

CHAPTER 6

*D*elilah might have laughed if she had the breath for it. Was she sure? No. A thousand times no. Agreeing to learn to swim, for fuck's sake, had been a ploy to separate Ry from his phone. Full stop. A little peep show to keep him distracted while she stole from him.

Nowhere in the plan was her ending up naked and on the verge of begging. If she was a different woman, she'd coldly use this to further her endgame of saving her sister. If she was a different woman, she'd have spared a single thought for that endgame in the last ten minutes.

Delilah wasn't that woman.

In the end, she was just as sinful and wanton as her father had always claimed, because she couldn't concentrate past the pulse of desire between her thighs. She licked her lips, giving herself over to the tableau they created in the mirror. He was so much bigger than she was, his body dwarfing her as easily as he held her in place in the water. The strength in his arms, of his chest against her back, of his legs pressing against hers …

This man was a weapon.

And all he wanted in this moment was to make her feel good.

To *taste* her.

Power flared, even headier than what she felt when she stepped on stage. She relaxed back against Ryu, letting her head rest against his chest. "I'm sure." She gripped the side of the pool, the faint pain reminding her not to let go, not to give into the temptation to touch him. "Make me feel good, Ryu."

He didn't ask again.

He simply held her gaze as his hand on her stomach descended out of sight beneath the water and cupped her pussy. No hesitation. No careful exploring. He touched her like he already knew her body intimately. Knew what she liked. Knew what would get her off.

Ryu worked two blunt fingers into her, filling her in a way that felt so good but was nowhere near enough, considering the size of his cock pressed against her ass. "I've thought about this," he murmured. "Every time you dance for me in the private room, I think about this."

There wasn't enough air in the room. "You think about fingering me?"

"I think about making you come." He gave her a startlingly rakish grin. "In a number of ways. Not just with my hands."

Oh god.

She was in so much trouble. So, so much trouble.

Delilah fought to keep her voice even, to not press against his hold on her stomach so she could fuck his hand. "Have you thought about me dancing on your dick?"

"Have *you*?"

She whimpered and tried to move, to create the friction she needed so desperately. "Ryu, please."

Just like that, his hand was gone. He lifted her out of the

water and followed her onto the concrete floor. Delilah didn't have a chance to wonder what the hell was going on because Ryu hauled her to the nearest lounge chair and pressed her back onto it. "Hands on the sides."

He spread her thighs and moved down so he was kneeling on the ground with his upper body on the chair between her legs. It put his mouth perfectly even with her pussy and … She whimpered. "Now you're really just teasing me."

"Tell me how it'd go." He breathed against her clit. "I won't stop as long as you keep talking."

It was official. The man was a sadist. She swallowed hard. "It starts off like we normally do … Ah!" She pressed her lips together hard as he licked up her center.

And then he stopped.

Right. Keep talking.

"I, uh, dance for you." He explored her with his mouth as if he had all the time in the world, as if this fantasy didn't have some sort of conclusion, as if it was more about his enjoyment than about getting her to come so he could move on to fucking. Delilah gripped the sides of the lounge chair so hard, her wrist spasmed. She ignored it. "I start on the stage, but it's different this time."

He paused. "Different, how?"

"You talk to me."

He leisurely circled her clit with this tongue. "Keep going."

"You wait until I'm down to my thong and then you crook your finger at me, beckoning me down to you. I'm not supposed to …, but I want to." She had no business fantasizing about this man, had *never* had any business fantasizing about him. Because he was her boss. Because he was dangerous in a way she was determined to avoid. Delilah might not have the most boring of jobs, but her life was pretty mundane otherwise. She preferred it that way.

There was absolutely nothing mundane about the man she'd known as Pestilence. She'd realized that even before they started down this path. A path that included him licking her pussy as if she was his favorite flavor of ice cream, his big hands bracketing her thighs, holding her open for him.

"I bend over in front of you … as I take off my panties." Usually at that point in the fantasy, she touched him. That part didn't work anymore. She cleared her throat, trying to concentrate on the story she spun, trying to hold off the pleasure building in waves.

Ryu flicked her clit with the tip of his tongue. Not enough pressure to get her over the edge, but just enough to bring her right to it. Delilah gasped. "That feels so good." She tried to focus. "You take your cock out. A clear invitation."

Keep talking, keep talking.

Don't do anything to make him stop.

"I, uh, climb onto your lap. I keep my arms up, hands clasped on the back of my neck. I'm already so turned on from dancing for you that I'm practically dripping. I *need* you." She bit back a moan and powered forward, her voice so breathy and low, it sounded like it came from another person. "I hold my breath as you guide your cock into me."

He lifted his head, his dark eyes gone hazy with wanting her. "Someday, you're going to do that."

"It's against the rules," she whispered. There was absolutely nothing Delilah wanted more in that moment than to do exactly what she'd described. To ride his cock, to work herself toward coming even as he watched her with the same expression on his face that he had right now.

As if she was the most wondrous gift he'd ever received.

Ryu gave her that same grin, the one that had her whole body clenching. "I think you like it more *because* it's against the rules."

Caught.

She licked her lips. "Maybe." Ryu released one thigh and pressed two fingers into her. Delilah gave up watching and closed her eyes. "Yes. Definitely."

He fucked her slowly with his fingers, exploring her until he found the spot inside her that made everything go hazy. "There you are." She opened her eyes as he dipped down and went after her clit again. Ryu experimented with his strokes, his dark gaze on her face all the while. It didn't take him long to find the right touch there, too.

It was too much. His fingers inside her, his tongue licking her just right, his attention like a living thing against her skin. Delilah's back bowed and she cried out as she came. He didn't stop, didn't slow down, didn't do anything but keep milking her orgasm from her. Wave after wave, until she could do nothing more than lie there and shake.

Only then did he slide his fingers from her. She half expected him to move up her body, to push to the main course, but Ryu never ceased to surprise her. He moved away from her clit, but he drew his tongue over her pussy in long, lazy licks, as if he couldn't get enough.

"Ryu?" she rasped.

"I'm not done yet." He hesitated. "Do you want me to stop?"

Did she want him to stop? Was that a trick question? Delilah's whole body had gone languid and disconnected, pleasure beating through her in slow waves. He touched her as if he couldn't think of anywhere he'd rather be. As if going down on her was the best gift he'd ever been given.

She'd have to wake up soon.

Wake up. Right.

That's all this was. Some kind of strange fever dream, a detour on her way to a destination she wanted nothing to do with. But reality could wait. Right now she was naked and had Ryu between her thighs, touching her as if she was something to be treasured. In this moment, he wasn't a man that borderline scared the shit out of her. He was a lover who wanted her pleasure above all else.

They'd go back to that, back to standing on opposite sides of the line. He would become Pestilence again and she'd be the woman on what sometimes felt like a suicide mission. But not right now. Not yet.

She licked her lips. "No, Ryu. I don't want you to stop."

His wicked grin made her stomach flip. "Good."

Her whole world melted in the pleasure he gave out with every slow slide of his tongue. She had no idea how long Ryu kept her there, drawing her close to orgasm again and again, each peak higher than the last, until he finally shoved her over the edge and she came screaming.

Screaming.

Delilah stared at the ceiling, trying to relearn how to breathe, to settle back into her body again. Seconds slid by, one after another, and she finally lifted her head. Ryu had his forehead pressed against her lower stomach and his hands clasped around her thighs tightly enough to anchor her in place. He was so tense, it was a wonder he didn't explode. "Ryu?"

"Give me a second."

Alarm dispelled some of her pleasure. "Are you okay?"

He gave a rough laugh. "I'm trying very hard to remember all the reasons I can't flip you over and fuck you right here on this lounge chair."

She nibbled her bottom lip. "Is there a compelling reason?"

"I promised that I would make you feel good."

"Your cock would make me feel *great*." God, what was she doing? She should be happy that all he wanted was so lick her pussy until she was a melted puddle of a woman. She shouldn't be pushing him for yet more.

He lifted his head. "I also don't have condoms."

Oh. *Oh.* She was gone for him in this moment, but not *that* far gone. Delilah had a short and fiery debate with herself, but she finally propped herself up on her elbows. "You asked my fantasy earlier."

"Yes."

"If sex is out of the equation …" She shivered. "If it's out of the equation, what's *your* fantasy." She saw the way his mind was going and rushed on. "Not to make me come half a million times. Hand jobs are out for obvious reasons."

"Agreed." The way he watched her had Delilah shivering again, as if she was a complicated puzzle box he'd take great delight in pulling apart and putting back together again.

She should stop, should let this end now, but her mouth kept moving and words kept emerging. "You love my tits."

"You have great tits."

Delilah cupped her breasts, making sure to spread her fingers so he could see her nipples. His gaze narrowed, just like it did when she touched herself while she danced for him. "Do you want to fuck my breasts, Ryu?" She loved the way his body went tight at every dirty word she said, as if he couldn't get enough of them. Of her. "You like to watch." She drew her finger down the center of her chest. "Watch your cock slide here, watch my nipples go tight with wanting you, watch yourself come all over my chest."

Dirty. So fucking dirty. She really was nothing more than a temptress, leading herself and others into sin. Delilah didn't care. She wanted him too much.

"Fuck," he breathed.

"Is that a yes?"

"That's a hell yes." He moved up her body and straddled her stomach. Delilah held her breath and Ryu shoved his swimsuit down his hips to free his cock.

It was even better than she'd imagined. Seeing was believing, after all, and Ryu's thick length took her breath away. She wanted him inside her, fucking away the last of reality clinging like stubborn cobwebs to her mind. It wasn't in the cards today, but this was the next best thing.

He fisted himself and gave a rough stroke. "Open."

Her body went tight as she obediently parted her lips and let him guide his cock into her mouth. Wetting himself on her tongue. Making a mess of both of them. She lost herself in the feeling of him carefully fucking her mouth. Why hadn't she suggested this in the first place? She kept her hands on her breasts, gripping herself tightly to resist reaching for him. She wouldn't do *anything* to stop this before its inevitable conclusion.

She couldn't stop a moan of protest when he pulled free, and Ryu's dark chuckle had her clenching her thighs together. "Another time." He braced himself on the top of the lounge chair. "Now."

Delilah pressed her breasts together and arched up as he slid his cock between them. It was so incredibly dirty. So wrong.

She loved every second of it. She watched Ryu's face, his expression twisted into something both awestruck and fierce. As if he couldn't believe this was happening. Well, that made two of them.

The power in each thrust had every muscle in his body flexing. She went a little lightheaded at the sight. She knew he was sexy, of course. Delilah *had* fantasized about taking things too far in the private rooms just like she'd told him. But this was different. Without his suit, he was all raw power and a concentration that left her shaking.

"*Delilah.*" He gave a shudder and then he came in great spurts across her chest and neck. She closed her eyes against the raw longing in his face. No matter how much she desired him, in that moment, she couldn't trust what he might see on her face.

He might see the truth.

She just didn't know *what* truth. That she was a traitor in waiting. That she wanted to flip him over and ride his cock just like she described early. That she didn't want to fuck him because she was a traitor. She wanted it *despite* that.

Oh god, what was she *doing?* Reality came crashing down around Delilah the second she opened her eyes. Sexing up Ryu wasn't part of the plan, and even if it had been, getting swept away remained out of the question. Except that's exactly what she did.

She sat up the second he moved off her. Now would be the time to grab his phone and do what needed to be done. Or it would be if Ryu wasn't staring at her like he'd come across an equation he couldn't quite unravel.

I've made a terrible mistake.

"I have to go."

"What?"

She scrambled off the chair, cast a look at the pool where her discarded suit floated, and gave it up for a lost cause. She could *not* think about the stickiness coating her chest—or how it didn't really bother her at all. "I have to go. Right now."

"Delilah."

She had to get out of that room right that second, because if he said her name again in that gentle tone of voice, she might throw herself at his feet and beg him to save her. Delilah knew better than to trust him—to trust anyone—to help her. Ryu might have the markings of not being a total monster, at least in this moment with lust clouding her brain, but the truth was she didn't know a damn thing about him beyond his reputation as Pestilence. If Pestilence found out that she planned to betray him, he'd toss her off the island. That was the *best-case* scenario.

If Death found out?

Well, she wasn't called Death without reason.

"I'll, uh, see you around." She couldn't think about how she was going to get access to his phone. The only thing that mattered was getting the hell out of there before she told him the truth and Esther paid the price. The Horsemen had no reason at all to care about Delilah's little sister. They wouldn't prioritize her safety.

That's why Delilah had to.

"Delilah, stop." All the softness had disappeared from his voice, leaving only the hard edge behind. The reminder of exactly who he was and why she couldn't trust him.

"I'm sorry." She grabbed a towel and winced as the move pulled at her wrist. When Ryu had his hands on her, she hadn't been thinking about the ache. She'd only thought of the pleasure. An apt metaphor, that. Pleasure would get her and the only person she cared about in this world killed. Pain was the only truth Delilah could trust.

"I have to go." She wrapped the towel around herself and bolted out of the room.

CHAPTER 7

*R*yu had well and truly fucked up. In all the years since they escaped that camp, he'd clung to the truth that he'd never hurt an innocent. Their enemies knew what they signed up for. So did the people who came to the Island of Ys to do more than throw away time and money. To move against the Horsemen was to invite retribution that was downright biblical in nature.

And yet in the last forty-eight hours he'd hurt an innocent woman.

Twice.

He dropped his head into his hands and cursed long and hard. It didn't help, but he hadn't really expected it to. Nothing helped anymore.

"Rough day?"

He looked up to find Luca standing in the doorway. The weeks of recovery from his injuries had taken their toll on Ryu's brother. He'd lost muscle mass and his once-suntanned skin was several shades paler from all the time spent inside. He even moved with a stiff way that indicated pain. For all that, seeing him up and moving after a period of time when

69

they weren't sure if he'd even live … It made Ryu smile. "You could say that."

"Want to talk about it?" Luca took several steps and carefully lowered himself into the chair near Ryu's desk.

"You escaped your nurse?" Cami had barely left Luca's side since he was injured. Their honeymoon period was spent in physical therapy, but she hadn't faltered once. He respected the hell out of her for that. His brother really had chosen well.

At his raised brows, Luca glowered. "Cami and Kenzie are off doing something they very carefully didn't talk about in front of me, and I figured it was better not to ask."

"Wise of you."

"I'm a wise kind of guy." He frowned. "But we're not talking about me. We're talking about what has you cursing into an empty room. Is this about the exotic dancer?"

For the most part, they kept no secrets from each other, but the flip side of that was that his siblings gossiped like old ladies. "I keep fucking up when it comes to her."

A faint smile ghosted across his brother's face. "I'm familiar with the experience."

"This isn't like you and Cami. She just …" He hesitated. To admit that Delilah gave him peace was to admit exactly how fucked up he was over the revelation about his father. He wasn't sure he wanted to talk about it, wasn't sure he *could* talk about it. Of them all, only Luca had come from a healthy home—at least before he was stolen. If it weren't for Ryu's father, Luca would have been raised in his home country, Thalania. He would be a lord, and he probably would still have ended up with Cami. She just wouldn't have had to renounce her role as Princess of Thalania in the process. Not to mention the abuses Luca suffered. Different from Ryu's, but no less harrowing. He had the physical scars as a reminder of everything he'd survived.

Too many sins to count, and all of them could be laid at Ryu's father's feet.

How could Ryu avoid feeling guilty about that? How could he unload his bullshit on Luca when *his* bloodline was the source of all their pain?

"It's not your fault."

He looked up to find his brother watching him closely. "What?"

"You're grappling with guilt that has nothing to do with you." Luca ran his hand through his dark hair. "Shit, Ryu. If anyone should be extra fucked up about this, it's you and Te. I was just some random kid. So was Kenzie. But he's your father and he knowingly put you in that place. You're entitled to your pain, but you don't get to add guilt to the shit you're already carrying around."

He wished he could believe that. "It's not that simple."

"It's exactly that simple." Luca gave a wan smile. "But neither you nor Te take things at face value, so that means you won't do it with this, either. We'll bring our special brand of justice to him. You can count on it."

He knew that. Of course he knew that. It just ... "It isn't enough."

"Nothing's enough." Luca shrugged. "But if you let this eat you alive from the inside, then it finishes the job they started in that place. And he wins." He leaned forward, dark eyes intense. "He doesn't get to win, brother. He didn't then, and he sure as fuck doesn't now just by virtue of his connection with you."

Luca was right.

Ryu just wished he could shrug off the sick feeling coating his skin so easily. "I'm losing it."

"You're dealing with some shit. It's temporary."

It didn't *feel* temporary. It felt like things spiraling out of control, a top spinning faster and faster beneath his feet.

71

Nothing remained solid. One wrong step and he'd be lost forever.

Wrong steps seemed to be the only ones he could manage these days.

"I hurt her."

Luca sat back. "From what I understand, it was an accident."

"We're too well trained to let something as simple as an accident fly and you know it." They each had their baggage. Luca couldn't deal with anything that took him back to those long hours and days in the icy forest, to the violence he was roped into there. Kenzie had to let off steam with fucking or fighting on the regular or she started to come a little loose around the edges. Amarante had her own ways of dealing with shit when the pressure got to be too much.

And Ryu?

Ryu worked.

He glanced at his computer. The puzzle that had intrigued and tormented him in equal measure for the last fifteen years was solved. The answers brought him no joy. They sure as fuck brought him no peace.

"Ryu." Luca shook his head. "I won't make excuses for you. You fucked up. But if I know you, you're going to make it right."

If only it were that easy. He couldn't get the panic on Delilah's face out of his mind. She hadn't panicked when he'd grabbed her wrist. Hadn't *really* panicked when they were in the pool. But their bringing each other to orgasm was enough to have her fleeing naked from the room.

"I fucked that up, too."

Luca huffed out a laugh. "This woman had you tied in knots."

"It's not that simple. I crossed the line." He ran his hands over his face. "I thought I'd teach her to swim."

"She lives on an island and can't swim?"

He almost laughed at the incredulity in his brother's voice. "That's what I said."

"So you started teaching her to swim. That's sweet, right?" He said it like he wasn't quite sure.

"It would be." Damn it, he had to say it. "I lost control again. I fucking mauled her, Luca. She gave me an inch and I all but fucked her right there in the pool."

Luca went still. "I'm going to need you to explain."

Even his brother didn't fully trust him. The confirmation of exactly what he feared shook Ryu more than he expected. "I didn't force her," he bit out.

"No fucking shit you didn't force her." He narrowed his eyes. "That is *not* what I meant."

Ryu swallowed hard. "I'm her boss. Maybe not directly, but ultimately I have the power to fire her if it comes down to it."

"Yeah. So?"

"So." He wanted to punch his brother a little in that moment. A lot. "She's injured because of me, she's out of work for over a week because of me, and then I'm panting all over her like some horny idiot and she's giving it up to me because she doesn't know what other option she has."

Luca stared for a long moment. And then he burst out laughing. "You are so full of shit."

"Goddamn it, take this seriously."

"I think you're taking it seriously enough for the entire island. Fuck, Ryu, I haven't met her personally, but even I know how Delilah Velásquez operates. That woman takes shit from no one—not even you. If she didn't want whatever went down between the two of you, do you think she'd be sending messages asking to see you?"

That brought him up short. "What?"

"Yeah, *what.*" Luca held up a square notecard. "Damien

passed this off to me." He held it out, and Ryu tried and failed not to snatch it out of his hands. A handful of words written in handwriting nice enough to pass for font.

Sorry.
Let's try this again? Tonight?

What did she have to be sorry for?

He set the card on his desk. "This changes nothing."

Luca sighed. "Fine. Be an idiot if that's what you're determined to do." He carefully leaned back and touched his side. "When is Te going to let us in on the plan she's putting together?"

Luca and Kenzie always did this. They assumed that Ryu had an inside thread into how Amarante's mind worked. He did in a lot of ways. His sister had been his one guiding light for as long as he could remember. She protected him in the camp as best she could. Later, when they were homeless in the streets, she'd taken charge and it was her plans that eventually got them out.

That and Ryu's technological know-how.

But with each step of this plan they enacted, Amarante grew more and more distant. The reveal that their father's hand held the reins had barely made her miss a step—at least on the surface. Even he didn't know what went on beneath her icy exterior.

Not this time.

Footsteps made them both look up as Amarante walked into the room. She took them in with a sweeping glance. "You'd be better served to ask *me* that question, Luca."

He snorted. "Kind of hard to do that when you're spending hours on end closeted up. Figured you'd take it badly if I kicked down your door."

"As if you could kick down anything in your current

condition." She raised an eyebrow. "But to answer your question, we talk tomorrow. It's time to lay out all the facts."

"Fucking finally."

Amarante turned to Ryu. She frowned. "You made it worse."

"I made it worse."

She rolled her eyes. "Go fix it, brother. You won't be able to focus until you do."

She spoke nothing more than the truth, but he couldn't help resenting how none of his siblings took this seriously. He'd fucked up. Significantly fucked up. Yet they kept insisting on acting like he had all the excuses in the world. As if he could do no real wrong. Misstep, sure, but not actual harm.

As if he didn't have the blood of a monster running through his veins.

Ryu rose and walked out of the room before they could roast him further. On another day, in another time, he'd enjoy the grief they handed out, would see it as further evidence of healing. There was a time when none of his siblings joked. Not even Kenzie.

But he couldn't appreciate it now. Not when their loyalty meant they continued to overlook the damage he'd done. He had to find a way to make this up to Delilah, and to do it without losing control. She deserved better than that.

If he was a better man, he'd leave her alone completely.

Ryu stopped short. That was the answer, of course. He couldn't trust himself around Delilah, which meant he couldn't *be* around Delilah.

The realization left a sour taste on the back of his tongue. Disappointment. Selfish dick that he was, he wanted to go around with her another time or two. The reaction, more than anything, spurred him into motion. He'd have to be back in the hub to meet with his siblings in the morning, but in the meantime, he needed to get the hell away from Pleasure and the temptations it offered by way of proxy to Delilah. His best bet would be to leave the island completely, but it wasn't an option.

Feeling confident in his plan for the first time in weeks, he headed for the exit. No matter how shitty it felt, staying away from Delilah was the best option for both of them. The money he'd deposited in her account would have to be apology enough.

Maybe he'd actually believe that, given enough time.

Maybe.

CHAPTER 8

*a*fter a day spent kicking herself for acting like the worst kind of fool, the fact that Ryu was apparently going to stand her up was just salt in Delilah's wound. She had one chance to get close enough to gain access to his phone, and she'd screwed it up.

She had to find a way to fix this before her sister paid the price.

She *couldn't* fix it if Ryu decided not to give her the time of day. Why would he? After all, she'd let him come on her chest and then left him with a whole hell of a lot of confusion. Most people didn't respond to mind-blowing orgasms by fleeing the room immediately after.

Delilah really, really hadn't wanted to flee the room. No, she'd wanted to follow through on the fantasy they'd spun around each other, to straddle him on that chair and ride his cock until he lost his damn mind.

More, some foolhardy part of herself had wanted to tell him the truth. About the threats against her and Esther. About what the man on the phone wanted.

She knew better than to take that risk, though. No matter

how he looked at her in the midst of fooling around, he was Pestilence. Maybe he hadn't hurt her on purpose, but there were others who weren't so lucky. The Horsemen might not hurt people indiscriminately, but they *did* hurt people. Like the guy who'd tried to cheat at blackjack. Or the male stripper who attempted to run a side business of fucking customers without doing it the sanctioned way—and giving the Horsemen their cut. Or ... The list went on. Every single person who crossed the Horsemen was made an example of, guest and employee alike.

Those people were just trying to mess with the business side of things. She didn't know what would happen to someone who actually went after the Horsemen directly like she was supposed to. They might not make an example of her. They might just disappear her completely.

Her phone rang and she startled. "Damn it, I need to stop doing that." It wasn't the secret phone. It was the landline to the room. Could it be Ryu? Her heartbeat picked up as she answered. "Hello?"

"He's in Pain. Wear something appropriate."

Click.

Delilah blinked. She knew that voice, even after only a handful of interactions. Why in the hell had Death decided to meddle with Ryu's affairs? Or, more accurately, why had Death decided that throwing Delilah at him was a legit course of action?

She knew better than to look a gift horse in the mouth, but Delilah couldn't guarantee that's what this was.

Maybe it's a set up. If *that* wasn't a thought to send her to her knees, she didn't know what was.

No.

Stop it.

Reason it through.

If Death had any idea what Delilah was up to, she'd deal

78

with it herself. She wouldn't lay some trap and wait for Delilah to walk into it. Not at the risk that Delilah might succeed. No, if this was a set up, it was a *set up*. As in she wanted to set Delilah and Ryu up.

She could sit here all night and wonder what the hell the other woman was thinking, wasting yet another of the days she didn't have ... Or she could do something about it.

In the end, her priorities came down to the same thing they'd almost always come down to—Esther's safety. Delilah would lie, cheat, and steal for her sister. She had before. She'd hoped that part of her life was behind her, but she didn't have the time or energy to worry about hopes and wishes.

In the end, there was only her reality. And her reality demanded she find a way to get access to Ryu's phone.

She dressed carefully for Pain. The other casino held a very different flavor to Pleasure, and though she'd been over there a time or two, it held too many temptations for Delilah to make a habit of it. Her priorities didn't include losing her annual income to a high stakes poker table, and she wasn't overly interested in fucking her customers, so she kept away from the play rooms. It wouldn't do to give someone the wrong idea. She'd just end up with a whole bunch of assholes thinking they were the exception to the rule.

They weren't.

No one ever was.

Until Ryu.

She finally settled on a tight high-waisted black skirt that was indecently short and a faux corset lacy crop top in cream. She mussed her hair a little and left it to fall in waves around her shoulders and touched up her red lipstick. There. That would do.

After a few seconds of contemplation, she took off the wrist brace and replaced it with a thick leather cuff that effectively covered the bruise and gave her a little support. Black heels finished the look.

Thirty minutes later, she walked through the doors of Pain with her game face in place. She barely made it three steps before a black man melted out of the crowded tables and gave her a brief smile. "How're you doing, Delilah?"

"I'm doing good." She nodded at Damien, the man who seemed to run a whole hell of a lot of the island. He answered to the Horsemen alone, and though she and he would never be friends—he was too professional for that—she had a healthy respect for him. "I'm eager to be back to work."

"No reason to rush healing." He nodded at the hallway leading deeper into the building. "He's in the private viewing rooms. Number four."

No doubt Death instructed him to tell her that.

Delilah opened her mouth to ask what Damien thought of this whole thing, but stopped the words before they fell from her lips. Damien might be a decent guy, but like every other employee on the island, he owed his complete allegiance to the Horsemen. If he knew what she planned, no amount of liking her would stop him from turning her in.

She just smiled. "Thanks."

"Delilah."

She stopped a step away. "Yeah?"

"No doubt you know what you're about, but ... be careful." He turned and disappeared back into the crowd around the blackjack table before she could formulate a response. Really, what was there to say? In another life, maybe she would be letting herself fall into whatever this was with Ryu. After all, she lived by the motto, the bigger the risk, the bigger the reward.

Ryu had *risk* written all over him.

She headed back toward the viewing rooms. They were set up similarly to the private dancing rooms in her club, but they were peppered throughout the halls. They gave her the rundown over what each room covered when she first arrived here, and what the payments would be if she decided to participate in anything that went down at Pain. She was on the Island of Ys to dance, though, so she hadn't taken them up on it.

Delilah stopped in front of a black door with a stylized four on it. She had absolutely no idea what she was walking into. Probably not an orgy—this was one of the smaller rooms, after all, and Ryu had his thing about being touched. Lots of touching in an orgy. She swallowed hard to keep a borderline hysterical giggle inside. No use in waiting out here longer. She wouldn't know what she was walking into until she crossed the threshold.

Taking one last deep breath, she turned the handle and entered the room.

It was smaller than she expected, just large enough to house a curved couch and a tiny bar in the corner. The couch was deep and large enough to fit a handful of people, but the only one occupying it was Ryu. He sprawled in the middle, his gaze on the massive framed window that looked into a second room. This one was better lit and held a huge bed. On the bed, there was a woman and two men. They hadn't gotten to fucking yet, but they were well on their way. All were naked and one of the men had the woman pinned against his chest while the other went down on her.

Delilah watched his head move, watched the way the second man clasped her to his chest to keep her thrashing still, watched him cup her breasts with two big hands. *Oh wow.* Her body went hot, and then cold, and then hot again. *This* was what got Ryu off?

She couldn't say that she blamed him.

Ryu turned and froze. "Delilah?"

This whole time, she'd been focused on getting to him,

ensuring that she didn't miss another chance to gain access to his phone. She hadn't really thought about how she'd play it once she was in his presence. Standing here in this dim room with an insanely sexy scene going down on the other side of the glass ... She didn't know what she was supposed to do. "Hi."

"Hi," he echoed. Ryu narrowed his eyes. "How did you find me?" He didn't seem particularly happy to see her. That should scare her, probably. It *did* scare her, but not because she thought he'd hurt her. He wouldn't, not without reason. No, the fear taking flight in her chest was at the thought of what would happen to Esther if she failed. She couldn't stand here and stare at him until he got fed up and kicked her out. This was her last chance. Her *only* chance, really.

Delilah set her shit aside. It didn't matter how scared and uncertain she felt. Those emotions were nothing new. She'd been feeling them her entire life. She shoved them down into a little box deep inside her and clicked the lock shut. A mental trick she'd learned a long time ago, one to keep her from losing her mind while she lived in her father's house. Ryu and her father might be nothing alike, but her helplessness in her current situation felt identical. It didn't matter. She'd gotten out before, and she'd find a way out now.

Delilah forced herself to stop worrying her bottom lip and speak. "You're avoiding me."

Ryu didn't blink. "Usually when someone is avoiding you, you don't seek them out like this."

A fair point, but she didn't let that dampen her momentum. "You're feeling guilty and out of control, and you're blaming me for it. That's not fair."

His glare intensified. "Am I feeling guilty, Delilah? Or am I getting mixed messages that I won't want anything to do with?"

Guilty. She had no ready response to that. Even without

the clock ticking down in her head, she would have dodged spending more time with Ryu. He was dangerous, for one. Maybe not dangerous to her, but she couldn't guarantee that. Not really. His first priority would always be the island and the other Horsemen. Even if he didn't rule the same way her father did, she'd had enough of being attached to powerful men in one way or another. It always worked out well for them.

Not so well for her.

Walking away wasn't an option, no matter how much she might prefer it. Something like relief flicked through her. She didn't have to walk away. She had no choice, so it was okay to take a step closer to this man. If only for a little while.

"You're punishing me for no reason." Brazen to challenge him like this, but she had to do *something* to ensure he let her stay.

He studied her for a long moment with a look on her face like he'd never seen her before. "You're acting like I went out of my way to hurt you by coming here. The last time we were alone, you *ran* from me. Most would call this respecting your wishes."

Now was the time when she'd spin some convincing lie to put him at ease, to weave the spell around them the same way she did when she danced. But when Delilah spoke, it wasn't a lie that spilled from her lips.

It was the truth.

"I don't do this." She motioned between them, encompassing more than just a stray orgasm in the pool. "I don't hook up with people I dance for, and my control doesn't slip, and I definitely don't put myself in positions that might negatively affect my livelihood. And what happened in the pool did all three of those things." He didn't speak, didn't move, didn't do anything but watch her with dark eyes, so she kept going. "I wanted what we did, Ryu. I wanted *more* than what we did. But it scared me, too." So many things scared her these days, the fear more deadly than water closing over her head, dragging her down to the deep.

He finally seemed to come to a decision and rose. "Do you want a drink?"

She wanted about ten drinks. "White wine would be great."

Several minutes later, she perched on the couch next to him. Close enough that he could touch her if he reached over, but nowhere near close enough to be seen as an invitation.

Liar. You being here at all is an invitation.

She still hadn't managed to look through the glass at the scene playing out on the bed. Delilah took a cautious sip of the wine. *Expensive.* It was dry and crisp and she could probably drink an entire bottle of it if she wasn't careful. She set the glass on the table near the couch. "I'm sorry."

"You have nothing to be sorry for."

If he only knew. She smoothed a hand down the soft fabric of the couch. "I'm the one who escalated things in the pool."

Ryu snorted. "We both seem determined to take the blame for the situation." He twisted a little and stretched his arm out over the back of the couch. An inch and he could brush his fingers along the bare skin on her shoulder. "There are a thousand reasons why I shouldn't touch you."

"Probably more than that why getting involved with you is a terrible idea." The way he pulled at her defied explanation. She caught herself leaning forward as if she was a flower seeking his sun.

"Getting involved," he said the words as if tasting them. "Delilah's a biblical name. The woman who seduced Samson and cut his hair."

A fact her father had reminded her of time and time again

as she grew up. As if he'd known the second her mother birthed her that she'd cause him nothing but trouble and decided to slap a name on her to justify his shitty treatment of her.

Temptress.

Heathen.

Sinner.

If he only knew.

She wanted to reach up and ruffle Ryu's hair, but touching him was out of the question. "I'm pretty sure Samson wasn't an innocent when he went into that relationship."

"No doubt." He gifted her with a grin, quick and wicked. The expression disappeared far too soon. "But I'm no Samson. I have responsibilities and, whether it feels like it or not, I ultimately hold power over your job. Over you. Losing control like we did before is it out of the question."

"Seems we both are coming up short on the self-control spectrum."

"Seems so." Something in him relaxed for the first time since she walked into the room. It left him seeming less like the forbidding Pestilence and more like a man. He went from dangerously attractive to something so much more. Ryu shook his head slowly. "What am I going to do with you, Delilah?"

She hadn't had a clear plan when she came into this room, but in that moment all Delilah wanted was have his hands on her again. To let him stop her circling thoughts in their tracks and—

That is not what I'm here for. Remember what I'm here for.

The phone.

Nothing more.

She took him in, telling herself she was searching for evidence of his phone. It wasn't the complete truth. Being able to drink her fill of this man was a reward all on its own. He always looked so perfectly put together in his black suits and white button-downs. Not a stray hair out of place. Not a button done up wrong. Even his shoes shone in the low light.

Except the closer she looked, the more she saw. He'd unbuttoned the top few buttons of his shirt, revealing a delicious slice of skin. The tiniest indication that he was here to relax, rather than to work. For all that, there was a tightness around his jawline and dark smudges beneath his eyes. He wasn't sleeping, and she had no idea if she was the cause or not. The thought that she might be made her a little sick to her stomach.

The knowledge that it would get worse if she was successful almost had her standing and leaving the room.

"Delilah." Ryu wound a strand of her hair around his finger. "I don't deserve your trust at this point, but I promise I'll do my damnedest to make sure this doesn't blow up in our faces."

If only it was that easy. Ryu might be one of the most powerful people in this little corner of the world, but the writing was already on the wall. He might like the way she looked, he might want to fuck her, but in the end she was disposable as far as he was concerned. Another one of the many employees that populated the island. She'd had her chance to come clean the second the phone showed up in her room. She hadn't then, and now she was complicit.

Getting banished from the Island of Ys was the very *best* case scenario, and that would mean the worst for Esther. And if Ryu or the others decided that her betrayal required a more permanent punishment?

Delilah couldn't guarantee that the man on the other end of the phone wouldn't hurt Esther out of sheer annoyance. No, she couldn't trust Ryu. Not with this. She couldn't let something as simple as guilt stop her from keeping her sister from harm. Delilah was a liar and, before this night was over, she'd be a thief, too.

The smart thing to do would be to turn the conversation elsewhere, or maybe to direct his focus to the threesome currently going on in the room on the other side of the glass. Distract him without letting herself become distracted in the process. But Ryu chose that moment to stroke his thumb across her cheekbone, the touch so light, she could almost convince herself she'd imagined it. She closed her eyes and leaned into the touch, willing to be swept away.

"You are so beautiful, it takes my breath away." The words came out low, as if he spoke to himself. "You quiet my demons, Delilah."

She opened her eyes. "Ryu." It was all there on the tip of her tongue. The truth. A confession. A plea for help, *any* help. But he was right. He hadn't earned her trust.

Not when Esther's safety hung in the balance.

She couldn't trust herself not to blurt it all out despite that, so she took the only avenue available to her. Delilah leaned forward and kissed him.

CHAPTER 9

*N*ow was the time to stop it.

To explain what Ryu meant when he said Delilah was beautiful, how he hadn't actually intended to seduce her. The second her lips touched his, however, all his good intentions went up in flames. He swore he could actually feel them turning to ash inside him. She tasted like cinnamon and something unknowable, as if he could spend the next ten years kissing her and never truly reach understanding of this woman. That, more than anything else, tipped Ryu over the edge.

He never had been able to resist a mystery.

Delilah was a fucking *mystery*. She never quite did what he expected, and she never reacted the way other people would in any given situation. It defied explanation, and he needed to know. Was it just the natural way she moved through the world, one of the few people who truly danced to a beat of their own drums? Was it all part of the wall she'd built up around her?

He didn't know, and because he didn't know, he sifted his hands through her long dark hair and tilted her head back to gain a better angle. Her tongue slid against his, as playful and wicked as the woman herself, and he groaned against her mouth.

The things you do to me.

Ryu wanted more. He wanted everything.

His sheer greed for her nearly overwhelmed him, but he managed to lift his head and break the kiss. Their ragged breathing mingled in the sparse space between them. It would be the easiest thing in the world to close that distance, to keep kissing her until things escalated beyond the point of no return. Until they both lost themselves yet again.

It wouldn't get him answers. Not really. She might give her body freely, but she kept large swathes of her inner self locked away from him. He had no right to ask for the key, but he wanted it all the same. "Delilah."

Whatever she saw on his face had her pushing to her feet. She looked … *divine* was the only word that came to mind. Her tight black skirt clung to her hips and ass, leaving nothing to the imagination and yet enticing him to see beneath all the same. It was barely long enough to be considered decent, giving the impression that one wrong move would give him a glimpse of paradise. The top of the skirt hugged the dip of her natural waist, and the tease of a shirt started a few inches higher. It was pale against her light brown skin, the boning making him think of a corset, but there was nothing confined about the way the piece of clothing offered her breasts up. Add in her just-been-fucked hair and sky-high black heels and his cock was so hard, he couldn't fucking think straight.

Delilah was temptation personified.

For one heavy moment, he thought she meant to flee again, but she turned a contemplative look at the room. "This isn't much different from the private room where I dance for you."

He saw where she was going with this, and found himself holding his breath. "You're not wrong."

"Ryu." She sounded like she was tasting his name, savoring it on her tongue. "Would you like me to dance for you *here*?"

He glanced at her injured wrist. There was no brace in sight, but she had a thick leather bracelet cuff covering the bruises. "You're hurt."

"No pole." She smiled, her dark red lips promising all sorts of delights. She glanced over her shoulder. "If you prefer the show they're putting on …"

"No." Not when his real life fantasy stood in front of him. He settled back against the couch and spread his arms over the back of it. "Dance for me, Delilah."

She gave him a surprisingly sweet smile and walked to the stereo system set up in the corner. A minute later, a slow throbbing bass line came through the speakers cleverly hidden around the room. It burrowed beneath Ryu's skin until it felt like his heart beat in time with the song.

Delilah let her head fall back as she began to move. It was both the same and completely different to when she danced onstage. She seemed to lose all awareness of the room around her, to become lost in the music and the pure joy that shone from her face with every sway of her hips.

It was as if he wasn't there at all.

His chest went tight and his cock hardened to the point where he felt a little lightheaded. His suspicion that she'd dance this way with or without an audience, that she trusted him enough to let that awareness of the space around her go, that instead of walking away at the end of this song, he'd get to touch her …

He could barely breathe past wanting her.

Delilah ran her hands through her hair and down her chest, cupping her breasts almost absently. Her lips parted and even though he couldn't hear anything over the music, he knew without a shadow of a doubt that a little gasp slipped free. She plucked at her nipples through the fabric of the top, but when that seemed not to be enough, Delilah reached behind her and unclasped it.

Each move felt like the most natural thing in the world, as if she'd play it out exactly this way even if he wasn't here. Ryu's mouth went dry and he leaned forward and propped his elbows on his thighs. A reminder to keep himself in place, to let her come to him.

The fabric of her top went slack and she hugged it to her a second before letting it slide down her arms and drop to the floor. She kicked it out of the way and it landed near the couch by his feet. Now nothing stood in the way of her questing hands, and she wasted no time touching herself again, rolling her nipples between her fingers until they stood at stiff points. All the while she kept up that slow grinding move, sometimes turning fully toward him, sometimes away, as if drawn to the sight of the two men fucking the woman and each other on the other side of the glass.

The beat of the song changed, becoming more insistent, and Delilah turned those dark eyes on him. She stalked to the couch, stopping just out of reach and running her fingers through her hair, pulling it back from her face and shoulders. She swiveled her hips and the fabric of her skirt rode up a little. Another half an inch and he'd be able to see if she wore any panties.

"Take off your shirt."

It took several seconds for her command to register. Ryu raised his brows, but he wanted to see where this was going. *Liar*. He *knew* where this was going. Had known it was coming from the point where she told him she fantasized about dancing on his cock. Maybe he hadn't expected it this quickly, but he wasn't about to complain. It reassured him in a way. As fractured as his self-control was, Delilah seemed to be right there in the free fall with him.

Whether they would crash and burn together remained to be seen.

He slowly unbuttoned his shirt and shrugged it off to drop on the floor with hers. Ryu made himself settle back against the couch and forced the tension from his body. Delilah obviously had a plan she wanted to enact, and he'd do whatever it took not to ruin it.

She turned around and pulled a move that had his body going tight. Delilah leaned back against him and rolled her body against his, her ass creating a delicious friction against his cock for half a second before she moved on, bending forward and reaching down to run her hands over her curves. "Do you want to touch?"

"You know I do."

"It's against the rules." She shot him a scorching look over her shoulder. "We shouldn't."

Even knowing this was role play, his cock went even harder. *Shouldn't* was such a sexy fucking word when it came from those red lips. "I know." She ground down against his cock again, and his breath caught. Fuck, everything about this woman made his breath catch. It was in the way she danced, in her confidence, in her devilish smile as she rolled her hips again.

She pulled a move that had her straddling him. "Maybe …"

"Maybe?"

She reached over his shoulders to hold the back of the couch and her lips brushed his ear. "Maybe if you take your cock out … Accidents happen."

Fuck.

"I'm no accident, Delilah." He loved the way her eyes hazed over every time he said her name. Like she couldn't get enough of this any more than he could. *"This* is no accident." He very deliberately bracketed her thighs with his hands and ran them up to the hem of her indecently short skirt. Holding her gaze, he inched the fabric up.

"Ryu," she whispered.

"Let me touch you." His thumbs brushed fabric and he looked down to find a tiny triangle of fabric shielding her from view. He traced the lines of it, enjoying the way her body went tense and still. "No one has to know that we broke the rules. It'll be our little secret."

* * *

DELILAH COULDN'T CATCH her breath. Not with Ryu idly stroking her through her panties. Sure as hell not when he cupped her pussy like he owned her. And he did. Just a little and just in this moment. She'd do damn near anything to keep this going.

"Touch me." The command came out hoarse with need.

"I am touching you." His lips curved.

"Touch me *more.*"

He tugged her panties to the side and dragged a single finger over her. "You're wet, Delilah. You like breaking the rules."

"Only with you." It was even the truth. Two years and she'd never once *really* wanted to cross the line, not until she started circling Ryu. She rolled her hips, but he easily moved back, keeping his touch devastatingly light.

Ryu gripped her hips and set her back on her feet. She stared, hurt rising, but it gave way beneath a cascade of need as he held her gaze and undid his pants, shoving them down enough to free his cock. He bent down and pulled open a compartment in the bottom of the couch. It was filled with condoms, and Delilah might have laughed if she had the breath for it. Instead, she watched, her heart hammering in her throat, as he opened the package and rolled the condom down his cock. Then he sat back and let her look her fill. He was beautiful like this, rumpled and watching her with those dark eyes, challenging her to meet him step for step.

Oh, she'd meet him all right.

Delilah shimmied out of her skirt and made a show of removing her panties. She left on the heels and turned around, letting herself roll backward down onto his body, rubbing against the same way she would in a normal lap dance. As if she couldn't feel his cock against her ass. As if she wasn't dying for him to fill her.

She turned as the beat changed and straddled him. "Just a dance."

The edges of his mouth pulled up. "Of course. Just a dance."

"Whatever happens … Happens." She braced her hands on the back of the couch and lifted herself up. Ryu didn't touch her with his hands, following the rules set out by the club, but he caught one of her nipples with his mouth and sucked hard enough that she moaned. She forgot what she was supposed to be doing and cupped her breasts, offering both to him.

He alternated, coaxing first one and then the other to stiff points. Delilah shivered and resumed her grip on the back of the couch. More. She needed more. She dragged her body against his, chest to chest, until she felt his cock nudge her entrance. "Just a dance," she murmured and tilted her hips, edging him inside her.

And, god, it wasn't enough. It felt so dirty and so right and so downright wicked as she impaled herself on him, inch by devastating inch, until he was sheathed completely inside her.

She leaned back and looked at Ryu. His entire body was

one long tense line, his muscles standing out against his skin as he obviously fought not to touch her, not to break the "rules."

Delilah reached for his hands and stopped, remembering their own rules. She hesitated, then arched her back. "You can touch my breasts if you want. That's allowed."

He palmed her breasts, seeming to learn her curves with the rough palms of his hands before playing with her nipples, pinching and teasing as she rode his cock. As she *danced* on his cock. It felt so fucking good. Better than she could have dreamed. *He* was better than she could have dreamed. "Yes, yes, yes."

"Touch yourself. Since I'm not supposed to."

She loved how committed he was to playing this game. How he followed the club's rules as if she wasn't about to come on his cock. She snaked a hand down to circle her clit, easily finding the touch that would send her hurtling over the edge. "I don't think there's a rule about orgasming in the private rooms."

"Then do it. Come for me, Delilah."

She stroked herself as she rode him, torn between wanting this to go on forever and wanting to reach the edge of pleasure that danced just beyond her grasp. Ryu made the decision for both of them. He hooked the back of her neck and towed her down to claim her mouth. He kissed her as she rode him and it was too good, too perfect. She came with a cry that he took into himself.

He lifted her and switched their positions, spreading her out on the couch and pounding into her as he chased his own pleasure. He was so beautiful like this, his powerful body moving in strong thrusts, his expression somewhere between agony and bliss. He came with a curse and slumped down next to her.

Delilah stared at the ceiling, trying to make sense of this

new world she occupied. She suspected sex would be world-shattering, but her imagination hadn't know the half of it. All she wanted to do was arch against him like a freaking cat and maybe eat a snack before they went for round two.

Her gaze tracked down to their pile of clothes on the floor. The pile of clothing that contained Ryu's phone.

Damn it, but she didn't have a choice.

She had to get his phone.

Now.

CHAPTER 10

$\mathcal{D}$elilah almost didn't take the phone. After what just happened with them, the desire to confess everything was stronger than ever. She knew better. Sex was something she'd never been able to separate from emotions, and just because she liked the way he fucked her didn't mean she could trust him with Esther. Even if Ryu—the Horsemen —decided not to remove Delilah entirely, they had no vested interest in her sister. To protect themselves, all they had to do was ensure Delilah didn't follow their enemy's orders. They certainly wouldn't launch an effort to keep Esther safe. She was just a girl to them. A stranger.

No, there was no other way.

She slipped into the bathroom touched the phone screen. To unlock it required tracing the correct pattern, but she'd seen Ryu do it once last week. Delilah held her breath and dragged her finger over the screen. Maybe he'd changed it since then. He seemed the type to update his security often.

It unlocked.

Feeling sick, she pulled up the messages app and typed out the number she'd been given. A few seconds later, the phone buzzed with an incoming message. A link to click that would no doubt give them access to all Ryu's information.

"Delilah?"

She jumped and almost dropped the phone. "One second." She clicked the link, waited a few seconds, and erased the message. She'd done it. It was over. She quickly dressed and tucked the phone into the pocket of his balled up jeans and walked back into the room. "Sorry, I grabbed your pants by accident."

Ryu stood in front of the glass, gloriously naked. The sight of him actually stopped her breath in her lungs. She set his jeans down and hesitated. Now was the time to make her excuses and get out. He was so tense, he obviously expected her to do exactly that. It left her feeling jagged and all sorts of tangled up. Better to meet his expectations now than to try to continue this farce.

Except it didn't feel like a farce when she was with him. It felt as natural as breathing. She'd told him things she'd never talked about before—not even with Esther. Oh, Delilah made sure her sister had a therapist as soon as she could afford one, but paving the way for Esther to heal was very different than sitting down and talking about all the horrible crap their father had done over the years. Better to leave it in the murky depths of the past, to ignore it between the times it rose and she had to beat it back.

Even without Ryu going into much detail about what he'd gone through, she felt a kinship there. They'd both survived. They'd both keep surviving, no matter what.

That connection had her crossing to stand in front him and smiling into the tension he was doing a piss poor job of hiding. "I wasn't running."

"I know." He turned and looked at her with a strange expression, as if he'd never seen her before. Her heart stuttered in response, but before she could think of something else to say, he kept speaking. "Have dinner with me."

The sheer *want* that rolled through her at his command nearly sent her to her knees. She wanted to spend more time with him—both in and out of bed. Giving into that temptation was a mistake. If it was just Delilah in the mix, she'd take her chances and go for it. But she wasn't the only person her decisions affected, and she'd never do anything to jeopardize Esther.

Maybe you shouldn't have slept with him, then.

She forced a smile. "Ryu, it's like four in the morning."

"Tonight then." He set his hands on her shoulders and ran them down her arms and back up again. "I'd like to get to know you better, Delilah."

She wanted to get to know him better, too. She wanted to dig into those little throwaway comments he'd made, to find out what made him tick, to just *know* him. It couldn't be, though. This whole thing started off ... Well, it hadn't started off as a lie. She'd felt the connection zing between them when she danced for him, weeks before that goddamn phone ever showed up in her room. If things had been allowed to play out naturally, then maybe it would be different.

Maybe a lot of things would be different.

Worrying about maybes and lost opportunities wasn't the road she wanted to travel into the future, though. She *didn't* want to keep up lying to Ryu, even by omission. She'd completed the task set out for her. The only thing she really needed to do was put some distance between them and stay clear of whatever the sick piece of shit on the other end of the line was planning.

What if they hurt Ryu?

She wrapped her arms around herself, suddenly cold. "We shouldn't spend more time together."

Ryu raised an eyebrow, something like amusement

lingering in his dark eyes. "Considering what we spent the last hour doing, I'd say that ship has long since sailed."

Hard to argue that, and if she kept resisting, he might stop to wonder why. Or that's what she told herself as she slowly nodded. "Dinner sounds nice."

He leaned down and pressed a surprisingly soft kiss to her lips. "No regrets."

She wished ... Delilah wished a lot of things. She gave him a small smile. "I promise I'm not bolting from the room." *Maybe just the island.* How long would she have to wait before she could go to Esther. *Should* she go to Esther? Talking to her sister on the phone might keep full on panic at bay, but she wouldn't truly draw a breath until she saw Esther in person. She had a shit ton of vacation time saved up.

Delilah almost laughed. Vacation time? Really? As if she'd ever be able to come back here. Even if Ryu never found out what she did, *she* knew. She would always know, and the guilt might choke her to death if she spent too much longer with him.

Ryu smoothed his thumbs over her cheekbones. "I'll walk you back to your room."

Something warm bloomed in her chest, but it was tainted by the truth. She might not have seduced him with the sole intention of getting to his phone, but she hadn't tried too hard to find another way.

Because you want him.

No shit, I want him. Who wouldn't?

They dressed in silence, and it took everything she had not to stare at the phone he pulled from their pile of clothes and tucked into his pocket. Was it in a different spot then where he'd dropped it? She couldn't be sure, just like she couldn't be sure if he'd noticed one way or another. They'd both been extremely distracted at the time.

The betrayal of what she'd done coated her throat like

acid, but she managed to dress and slip on her shoes without collapsing into a tearful confession. Instead of leading her to the front entrance, Ryu used his hand on the small of her back to guide her around to the side entrance of Pain. There, a cart waited for them.

As they drove back to Pleasure, she wrapped her arms around herself. "I hadn't meant this to happen when I tracked you down tonight. I mean, obviously I wasn't opposed to it happening, but I didn't *plan* on seducing you."

"Delilah." He waited for her to look at him to continue. "You seduce me just by breathing."

Her jaw dropped. "You can't say things like that."

"It's the truth." He shrugged in a way all the Horsemen seemed to—like it meant everything and nothing at all. "I had every intention of keeping our interactions confined to the club and following the rules there. Obviously, it wasn't meant to be." His hands tightened on the steering wheel. "If I was a better man, I'd leave you alone. But I'm not. I'm just selfish enough to keep you."

Keep you.

She couldn't breathe. "Ryu, you *really* can't say things like that."

"We'll talk more at dinner." As if it was already decided.

She couldn't dredge up words the rest of the way to Pleasure. What was there to say? He couldn't keep her because she was a traitor. She couldn't stay close to him because there was every reason to think his enemies would use that connection. Delilah knew how this worked, no matter how much she wanted to pretend it was over the second she clicked that link on his phone. If his enemies thought she meant something to him, they would use that connection.

They would force *her* to use that connection.

The burning in her throat crept up toward her eyes. It would be so much easier if she didn't like Ryu, if he was the kind of monster that so many people believed the Horsemen to be. But she was starting to realize that he wasn't monstrous at all.

She had to hold it together. She didn't have any other choice. Delilah pulled on damn near a decade's worth of playing a role and smoothed out her expression. "At dinner, then." She barely waited for the cart to stop to step out. "I'll walk the rest of the way myself. No need to go out of your way." She hurried away from him and into Pleasure before he could call her back.

It was only when she closed and locked the door to her room that she sank to the floor and let the tears fall. To be so close, to see exactly how this could play out if they were left to their own devices …

God, it hurt.

It hurt so much more than she expected.

The tears came faster, until she gasped for breath and pressed her hand to her mouth to keep the sobs inside. It took several seconds for her to realize the sound she heard wasn't internal. Delilah lifted her head and pressed her lips together. Yes, that wasn't in her head at all.

The phone beneath her mattress was ringing.

"No," she whispered.

She knew better than to ignore it. Delilah staggered to her feet and crossed to pull the phone out from its hiding spot. The now-familiar number taunted her from the screen. She really, really didn't want to take this call.

She slid her thumb over the screen. "I did what you asked. Leave my sister alone."

"Aw, Delilah, you know better." Even when he sounded happy, his voice still made the hairs on the back of her neck stand at attention. She'd survived on her own too long to ignore her body's instinctive response.

"I sent the text."

"You did." He laughed, low and harsh. "That was well played. You just bought yourself another week."

The room swam around her. "A week? What are you talking about?"

"Our boy Pestilence has taken a real shine to you. Keep doing what you're doing. Keep him happy. In a week, I'll call again with your instructions." The amusement bled out of his tone. "I don't have to tell you what will happen if you ignore my call."

No, he didn't have to tell her. He'd hurt Esther. She pinched the bridge of her nose and tried to *think*. Could she get to her sister inside of a week and convince Esther to … To what? To leave New York, to drop out of school and go into hiding? Esther had a whole life set up, one she'd worked too damn hard to abandon just because Delilah chose the wrong place to work and caught the attention of the wrong man. Even if Esther was willing, even if she could get to her sister without anyone noticing …

"You're thinking about running."

She pressed her lips together. Hard. "Of course not."

"That's good, Delilah. That's really good." He lowered his voice. "If I see you get on a plane, your little sister might suffer from an unfortunate accident. New York isn't the safest place, after all. A thousand different tragedies could befall her."

Her stomach lurched. How did this man get his information? He knew everything she'd done, everywhere on the island she'd gone, even when she and Ryu were alone. Maybe he didn't have someone on the inside at all. Maybe he'd somehow hacked the system …

In the end, it didn't matter. He had the one threat that would ensure she did anything he asked. No matter how horrific.

She closed her eyes, but it didn't relieve the burning. If anything, it got worse. "I understand."

"That's good. That's really good." He laughed. "Enjoy your week."

She couldn't shake the feeling she'd just sold her soul to the devil.

And he got a hell of a bargain.

* * *

RYU BYPASSED the hub and walked directly to his suite without talking to anyone. He locked the door and pulled his phone out of his pocket.

The same phone that Delilah swiped when she went into the bathroom earlier. He'd almost missed it, had been so blissed out on what they'd just been doing that he wasn't paying attention. If she hadn't shot him an almost guilty look before she shut the door, he wouldn't have investigated ...

But he did.

So here they were.

It took 10 seconds to find the backdoor she'd created, probably by clicking a link in a text message. He moved to shut whoever it was out ... Stopped. If he moved defensively now, whoever it was would know he was onto them. They might rabbit, and then he'd lose what little leads he had. Yes, he'd still have Delilah as a potential source of information, but even now Ryu had a hell of a time believing she'd worked here for two years without fault and suddenly become a spy.

Especially when she was so shitty at it.

No, this reeked of being in the wrong place at the wrong time. It didn't take a genius to figure out what leverage they used, either. She practically had a neon sign flashing over her head every time her sister came up.

Ryu grabbed his personal laptop and did a quick search.

By all accounts, Esther Velásquez was still living a normal life in New York, attending school and laying low. It would take him a few hours to dig deeper and see if she had anything to do with this mess, but he didn't have the time right now.

He sighed.

Delilah should have come to him the second she realized how in over her head she was. She had no reason to trust the Horsemen, even though they had a long history of protecting their people. That history wouldn't mean shit to her. Not when it came to her little sister. Her instincts to protect Esther were too ingrained, just like her belief that she couldn't rely on anyone but herself—not really.

So, no, he wasn't surprised that she'd tried to power through this clusterfuck alone, but hell if it didn't sting.

Ryu shut his laptop and set it aside. There was nothing to be done for the time being. He would switch out phones and keep a few texts and calls going out on the compromised one in order to maintain appearances, to play the clueless idiot until their enemy decided to make their move. Because there *would* be a move. Whoever this was didn't go through all this trouble just to get access to a phone.

Whoever this was. Ryu almost laughed. He knew who was responsible. If not by personal action, then at a least by giving the order.

His father.

Which meant it was doubly important that he not tell Amarante about this development. She might have all the appearance of being as calm and collected as ever, but he couldn't trust her reactions would reflect that. Especially to a threat that rose from within their ranks. The double betrayal would fuck his sister up, and she'd haul Delilah out to the third little island that they only used when they had ill deeds to accomplish. Amarante would torture her, and she wouldn't believe that Delilah didn't know anything.

105

No, there was a better way to play this.

He dropped his head into his hands and let loose a rough laugh. A better way to play this? More like he didn't want to admit that he'd started to feel things for Delilah he'd never felt for anyone before. He didn't want her to be the cold and calculating enemy that his sister would make her out to be.

In short, he was compromised. He just wished he could give a fuck.

There was a better way around this. He just needed some time and space to figure it out, which was shitty because time and space where two things he didn't have nearly enough of.

A knock on his door brought his head up. "Yeah?"

Amarante stepped into his room. To anyone outside their little circle, she'd seem just as put together as ever, but he'd known her his entire life. Ryu saw the exhaustion and worry she tried to conceal from him. And he saw the deep well of rage she didn't bother to hide. She closed the door and leaned against it. "For someone who spent a night with the woman he's been pining over for months, you don't look particularly relaxed."

"Like you would know." The sharp words escaped, and then there was no calling them back. Ryu sighed. "Ignore me. I'm just tired."

But Amarante, being Amarante, wasn't about to let him off the hook so easily. She tilted her head to the side, her long black hair flowing over her shoulder. "I wouldn't know what relaxation looks like? Or I wouldn't know anything about fucking someone I care about all night?"

"Damn it, Te." He shook his head. "I'm sorry, okay? Everything is backwards right now, even things with Delilah. It's not simple, and it's not easy, and it's messing with my head." He held up a hand. "But that's no reason for me to take it out on you. I'm sorry."

For a second, he thought she might push the issue, but her

shoulders dropped a fraction of an inch. "We're all wound too tightly right now."

"You can say that again."

She walked over and dropped down onto the bed next to him. "It's going to get ugly, Ryu. Really ugly."

"I know." He leaned his shoulder against hers, offering the only comfort she'd accept. "We'll get through it. We always get through it."

"Maybe not this time." She shook her head before he could question those cryptic words. "Let's go. Chances are we'll have to haul Kenzie out of bed with her Irishman, but Luca and his princess are already in the hub."

Luca and his princess.

Kenzie and her Irishmen.

Their tiny family was a little less tiny now, even if none of the new bonds would ever be as strong as the original ones. Somehow it didn't matter. Liam and Cami made life better, and not only because they made his siblings happy. They represented a future that might extend past this vendetta.

He just wished he could look into that same future and see something like their happily ever after for himself. Instead of an asset who was determined to do whatever it took for the sake of love, he'd gone and lost his mind over a woman who showed all evidence of being a traitor.

An *active* traitor.

"Ryu?"

He pushed thoughts of Delilah away. Amarante couldn't divine thoughts, but she read people well enough that she might as well be able to. "Yeah?"

"We'll get through this."

"I know." He wished the words didn't feel so much like a lie.

CHAPTER 11

*a*n hour later, the inner circle of the Island of Ys took their places in the main room of the hub. Six now, instead of their original four. All were uncharacteristically quiet as Amarante paced in front of them. Ryu studied his siblings' faces, finding no evidence of wanting to turn from their course. Both Liam and Cami seemed just as resolute.

It should have made him feel better. This was what they'd been working toward for so long, after all. They couldn't afford a stumble or second-guessing or anything that might draw them away from finishing this once and for all.

Like knowing that someone wanted to spy on them and keeping it to themselves. Like not sharing that Delilah was compromised.

Amarante stopped and turned on her heel to face them fully. "You're not going to like this."

Everything in Ryu went still, all his tangled bullshit over Delilah disappearing in an instant of perfect clarify. "What did you do, Te?"

She smoothed her hands down her red silk shirt. "We are going to have a summit, of sorts."

"A summit." Luca leaned forward and winced when the move pulled at his injury. "We agreed to plan together. Organizing a *summit* without talking to us? Are you out of your fucking mind?"

"You will cease reacting until you have all the information." She didn't raise her voice, but she didn't have to. There were too many times in their past when her orders saved them. Even now, as adults, they responded to *that* tone. "I didn't plan a summit. I am attending one."

The distinction clicked into place. Ryu shot to his feet. "No. Absolutely not. You're not leaving the island." They all left from time to time. It was unavoidable, especially when hunting their enemies. But she wasn't talking about a hunt. She was talking about putting a target on her forehead.

She shot him an icy look that had him dropping back into his chair. "We'll never reach him without drastic measures. You've seen the facts, the schematics, the schedules. We could spent the next ten years trying to plan the perfect assassination, and it wouldn't matter because he has enough enemies to be paranoid when it comes to his security."

"We'll find a way." This from Kenzie, who'd been strangely silent until now.

"If we could find a way, Ryu would have done it by now." Amarante flung a hand in his direction.

Everyone's attention turned to him. He wanted to say something to contradict his sister, but he couldn't lie. Not about this. "He's protected himself from threats both physical and digital. I can't get to him, and his travel schedule is so randomized, without someone on the inside, it's nearly impossible to anticipate with enough time to stage an assassination."

"So it will take time," Luca said. "That's fine. We have time."

"No, we don't." Amarante stalked to the nearest desk and perched on the edge of it. "You want to start a family."

He startled and winced again. "That's something we've only talked about in theory." Luca shot an apologetic look over his shoulder at Cami, but she shrugged. She always seemed to roll with the punches being in love with a Horsemen brought. It was one of many things that made Ryu respect the hell out of her.

"You cannot bring children into this world while he still breathes." She held up a hand before Luca could start in on her. "Don't you dare act like I'm forbidding it. I'm not. I'm stating a fact. Children might be innocents, but they're cannon fodder to someone like Fai Zhao. We know that better than anyone. I will *not* have my nieces and nephews raised in fear."

Cami cleared her throat. "We're a few years out yet, Amarante."

"The fact remains. It could be years and longer before we get access to him. It's an unacceptable timeline." She crossed her arms over her chest. "Which is why I accepted an invitation to the summit being hosted in one month's time at the Warren."

The Warren.

Ryu's breath left his body in a rush. "Then it's pointless. You can't touch him while you're there." The Warren was a very specific kind of business with a very specific kind of owner. Hotel and resort and stage all acted as a cover for one of the few neutral territories in the world. Its owner, Nicholai, had a reputation for hosting the most dangerous people their world could offer and allowing deals to be made without anyone finding a knife in their back in the process. At least a physical one.

When the Warren first came into being, people still thought they could break the rules. It had only taken

Nicholai making examples of three of them before people stopped testing him for the most part. Every few years, though, someone got it into their head that they could break the rules of neutral territory. None of them survived.

Amarante's lips curled. "I never was that good at following the rules."

"He'll kill you," Ryu whispered. There was no other outcome. People didn't cross Nicholai. The only thing he cared about was his neutral territory, and he made examples of anyone who breached that agreement. No matter how long it took to track them down.

Staying on the island might keep her safe for a while longer, but eventually someone would get to her. Their defenses weren't foolproof—Delilah was more than enough evidence of that. Eventually Nicholai would get to Amarante, and then he'd make an example of her just like he made examples of anyone who broke his rules.

Another shrug. "Everything has its price."

"No." He shot to his feet again. "Absolutely fucking *not*. You don't get to play martyr. He doesn't get to take *you* from us, too."

"Better me than any of you."

Now Kenzie was on her feet, too. "Fuck that and fuck you for even suggesting it. We can't get to him immediately? Fine. We'll figure out another way." She ran her fingers through her long blond hair. "I can't believe I have to keep talking you and Ryu off the fucking ledge. He is *not* a reflection of you, and you aren't responsible for what he did. You don't get to punish yourself for what happened in that place. *Neither* of you do." She cursed long and hard, her hazel eyes snapping. "If I have to tie you down until further notice, I'll damn well do it. You know I will."

Luca looked like he might be sick. "You really think I'd ask that of you? That I'd take my happiness at the expense of your life? What the hell, Te? Just … What the fucking hell?"

Ryu could actually feel his family fracturing around him. Kenzie kept threatening to tie Amarante down, getting more and more creative with her methods the angrier she got. Luca looked like he couldn't decide whether to throttle Amarante or throw his lot in with Kenzie and lock her up. Liam and Cami wisely kept out of it, though both them look concerned.

"Enough!" He didn't realize he intended to speak until his bellow silenced their fighting. Ryu met each of their gazes in turn and lowered his voice. "That is enough."

"Ryu—"

He pointed at his sister. Of them all, he knew what drove her. She might not acknowledge the guilt their bloodline brought, but he felt it right down to his marrow. His sister was not fatalistic, and if they forced her to slow down long enough, she'd find a better way forward. He needed to give her reason to slow down. "I need a week."

She tossed up her hands. "You've had several and haven't made any meaningful progress. What is one more week going to accomplish?"

"A week, Te. I'll find a better way forward, and you *will* respect that plan." He gave the barest of pauses. "I want your word."

"Ryu, no."

"Your word, Te. Give it or I let Kenzie and Luca tie your ass up and lock you in a room until we figure out an alternative course."

"You wouldn't dare," she snarled.

Kenzie took a step forward. "You know I damn well *would* dare."

"Fine! You get a week. Not a single hour more." She shoved off the desk and stalked away.

Silence reigned for several beats. Kenzie turned to Ryu and propped her hands on her hips. "Okay, we have a week. Now what?"

"I'll take care of it." In the end, there was only one string to pull. Delilah. He didn't even know beyond a shadow of a doubt that his father was behind her betrayal. The Horsemen had made quite a few enemies over the years, and it could easily be one of them who'd taken exception. Ryu didn't believe that, though. The timing was too coincidental to *be* a coincidence. That said, he knew better than to tell his siblings about her. Even now.

Especially now.

With fear for Amarante driving them, they'd do whatever it took to ensure her safety. They'd hang Delilah for the information, and happily.

No, Ryu had to find a balance that would find him answers and save his sister, which meant he was the only one who could do it. And it had to be now. If he had a week to get answers, he couldn't afford to waffle for even an hour. He turned and strode for the exit.

"Where are you going?" Luca called after him.

"I said I'll take care of it, and I will."

Even knowing time was of the essence, he still took a detour out to the low cliffs on the backside of Pleasure. They kept the guests to the inner island and the beach in the inlet, so very few people wandered out on this side of the building. He usually didn't come out here during the day, preferring to sit against the outer wall and look at the stars on clear nights. But the soft shushing sound of the ocean usually soothed him and brought a kind of clarity that sitting in front of a computer for hours on end could fuzz.

It didn't work today.

He looked out over the sun glinting off the water and all he could think about was the fact that Delilah couldn't swim.

A few reckless mental steps would put him right back in the pool with her. Had she intended her betrayal even then? She must have.

Surprising how much that hurt. The jagged pain in his chest only increased with time. He'd been intent to let this play out until he could find a way to talk to her, but that wasn't an option any longer. Seven days. He exhaled slowly. Seven days was a small eternity or a blink of the eye. He already knew how this would go.

Blink of the eye.

He had to move now. Ryu scrubbed his hands over his face. He could use a shower and six hours of sleep, but both would have to wait. The conversation with Delilah happened now.

Whether they were ready for it or not.

* * *

DELILAH COULDN'T SLEEP. She'd thought succeeding in her task would bring a sense of relief, but all that remained was an impending feeling of doom. She'd assumed it couldn't get worse. It almost made her laugh in the here and now. Couldn't get worse? She knew better. Every time she'd let herself fall into that lie while she was a child, tucking it around herself like a threadbare blanket, her father had gone and proved her wrong.

Every. Time.

She'd been on her own too long; she was out of practice. Instead of focusing on survival at any cost, she'd let herself fall into the belief that this threat would pass. She had no exit strategy in place. It didn't matter that they probably would have reacted the same way if she tried to leave the island before now. What mattered was that she hadn't even thought to try. Not really. She'd been too busy trading off cowering in fear and tripping over her own feet with lust.

The irony wasn't lost on her.

She'd spent eight years dealing in the very lust her father accused her of cultivating. Maybe it started off out of desperation and the need to give him the middle finger in the only way she knew how. Defiance. Eight years of cultivating lust in others and only allowing herself little sips to keep the dragon at bay. She should have known that it'd bite her in the ass at the most inopportune of times.

A knock on her door stopped her runaway thoughts in their tracks.

She crossed to it, but stopped before she touched the lock, silently debating with herself. Letting anyone in at this point was just adding to the potential clusterfuck. She was tired and sore and emotionally bruised. She didn't have the wherewithal to put on a mask and play to expectations.

"Delilah."

Ryu.

She closed her eyes and leaned her forehead against the cool wood of the door. "It's seven in the morning. Dinner isn't for another twelve hours."

"Let me in, Delilah."

Something in his voice had red flags waving inside her. She opened her eyes. "I'm really tired. Can we raincheck?"

"No." The lock flashed green and clicked open, which was the only warning she got to scramble out of the way before Ryu pushed the door open and stepped into the room. She opened her mouth to tell him off, but the words stalled somewhere south of her throat.

In the two hours since she'd seen him last, something had changed. This wasn't the intense man she'd spent so much time with over the last couple days. This wasn't even the sexy partner who'd dominated their bed games.

No, this was *Pestilence.*

Delilah took a step back before she could stop herself, and something like pain flared in his dark eyes. Ryu shook his head and locked her door. "Don't look at me like that."

"You just came into my apartment uninvited and now you're locking yourself in here with me. I don't think you get to tell me how I should or shouldn't look at you."

He stopped short, some of his coldness ebbing away. "That's fair."

"Thank you, Ryu, for telling me something I already know." She could hear the strident tone in her voice, could hear the anger covering up the fear, but she couldn't stop it. "I'd like an explanation."

"That makes two of us." He motioned at the kitchen. "You have coffee?"

"Not for you." She bit her bottom lip. Hard. *Get a hold of yourself.* Delilah propped her hands on her hips. "I'll put a pot on. You talk."

He nodded. "Okay."

She didn't trust this agreeable Ryu any more than she trusted the man who'd walked through her door with all sorts of retribution written across his face. Something was going one, and she couldn't pretend it had nothing to do with her. He obviously had found something out, whether it was on his phone or by other means. He'd just as obviously decided to come talk to her himself, rather than hauling her in for questioning or however the Horsemen usually handled this sort of thing.

Questioning. Torture. Murder.

You're spinning out.

Stop.

Breathe.

Focus.

She carefully measured out her scoops into the filter and

then filled the coffee pot with water. The focus didn't stop her hands from shaking, but it helped calm her thoughts. A little. "Why are you here, Ryu? Why like this?"

"Why did you take my phone?"

"What?" Her fingers went slack and she dropped the coffee pot.

Ryu caught it before it hit the floor. He set it on the counter and turned her to face him. She had the vague notion to resist his hand on her shoulder, but Delilah couldn't seem to form coherent thought. They stood there, close enough to kiss, and she might as well have been looking at a stranger. Ryu hid his feelings more effectively than she ever had. "Why did you take my phone, Delilah?"

To lie or not to lie? She didn't know. She just didn't know. "Ryu ..."

"The truth." No forgiveness there for her in his dark eyes.

If she gave him the truth, what would he do with it? Delilah didn't know. She wanted to see his presence in her apartment as a good sign, as some indication that she could trust him. If it was just her life in the mix, maybe she could. It wasn't just her, though. Esther's safety hung in the balance.

Her *life* was on the line.

She took a ragged breath and lowered her eyes. She couldn't guarantee what they'd show him. "I don't know what you're talking about."

"Damn it, Delilah." He touched her chin with a single finger, lifting her face up. "Don't make me do this."

If he killed her, what would happen to Esther? The Horsemen wouldn't hurt her. She believed that with her entire being. The man on the other end of the phone, though? She couldn't be sure, but he'd have no reason to. Esther was leverage. If Delilah died, she wouldn't serve as leverage anymore and they'd have no reason to hurt her.

The thought of death shouldn't bring her so much peace.

She met his gaze directly. Some of the steel bled back into her spine. "I don't know what you're talking about," she repeated. If it was just her … No point in thinking like that. It wasn't just her. It hadn't ever been just her.

Ryu closed his eyes for a long moment. When he opened them, there was no mercy to be found. "So be it." He took one step back and then another. "Get your things."

Alarm flared despite her determination to meet her fate calmly. "What?"

"Until you tell me the truth, you are no longer an employee of the Island of Ys." His tone was bored and distant. So, so cold. "You're also not a guest."

She stood there, feeling very small and vulnerable. "You're kicking me off the island?"

"And let an unknown threat loose?" He shook his head sharply. "No." Ryu motioned at the room. "Get the things you can't bear to part with, Delilah. You have five minutes."

She didn't ask for clarification again. If he planned on killing her, would he have her gather her things? Delilah didn't know. Because she didn't know, she didn't question the order. She simply walked to her closet and pulled out the bag tucked into the back that she'd stashed there for emergencies. A holdover from her and Esther's initial days on the run. They never knew when they'd have to bolt in the middle of the night. Their father didn't pursue them for long, but the threat of him was enough to keep their instincts sharp. Later, there were other dangers, other reasons when it paid for them to have an exit strategy in place.

Eight years later, and she was still prepared to flee from danger instead of fight.

She tried not to think about that too hard.

Delilah didn't spare a glance at the spot where she'd hidden the phone beneath the mattress. Either they'd find it or they wouldn't. If they did, she'd just claim ignorance. It wouldn't work any more than her denying messing with Ryu's phone, but she had to hold firm.

Esther's life depended on it.

Ryu's expression didn't change when she stopped in front of him. He just gave a short nod. "Don't do anything stupid."

Too late.

The hysterical thought had a laugh bubbling up her throat. She managed to smother it at last moment, but it was a close thing. Don't do anything stupid? Like get pulled into some plot against four of the most dangerous people on the planet? Like sleep with Ryu even though she knew she'd have to betray him? Like still wanting to tell him the truth even though she knew it was the worst mistake she could make?

She kept her lips pressed together as she follow him down the hallway to a side door. It led out to a patio and short dock that employees used to smoke and sun themselves, depending on the time of day and season. She stopped short at the sight of a boat bobbing next to the dock. "You lied."

"*I* didn't." He pressed a hand to the small of her back, moving her forward despite the way she dug in her heels. "We're not leaving the island."

"That's a boat."

"Yes, that's a boat."

Realization washed over her and her knees went weak. "You're going to take me out on the water and throw me in."

"*What?*"

She pressed a hand to her mouth, the world going hazy. "Just an accident, right? It's not your fault that I couldn't swim."

"Jesus, Delilah." Ryu grabbed her shoulders and turned her to face him. He didn't look cold right then. He looked furious. "I'm not going to murder you."

"Why not? You think I'm a traitor."

"You *are* a traitor." He said it with such surety, she

thought she might be sick. "That doesn't mean I'm going to murder you in cold blood."

"Just a little hot-blooded murder, then." A hysterical giggle escaped. She couldn't seem to stop talking. All these years of learning to control herself and faced with the very real possibility of her death at the hands of Ryu and she'd completely lost her shit. "Fine. Go ahead. It's not like I don't deserve it, right?"

CHAPTER 12

*T*here was no point in continuing this conversation. The longer they stood there, the greater the chance someone would see it and wonder why Ryu was having an argument with a clearly upset Delilah. Employees wouldn't interfere, but they'd contact Amarante, and *she* wouldn't hesitate to get involved. He had to get Delilah away from here before that happened.

Ryu wouldn't take her out and toss her to a watery death. He couldn't promise the same when it came to his sister.

With nothing left to do, he grabbed Delilah and tossed her over his shoulder. The only way this would work was if he got her out of here. Now. He took the trail down to the boat at a reckless pace and dumped them both into the little craft. It wasn't meant for the open sea, which was fine because he'd been telling the truth—he had no intention of taking Delilah from the island.

He just needed to get her away from this part of it.

Delilah stopped sputtering the second he got the engine going. He hated how she watched him, her dark eyes wide and terrified. She truly thought he'd drown her, and damn if that realization didn't make him sick to his stomach.

If she was anyone else, it wasn't out of the realm of possibilities.

His hands weren't clean. They hadn't had a chance to *be* clean, not when he grew up in Camp Bueller, not when they escaped and had to fight tooth and nail for every little thing for years. Not when they'd set out on this path to bring down their own personal bogeyman. He wished he could blame all those actions on the person who put him down the path in the first place, but Ryu had worked too hard for freedom to do anything but take responsibility for his actions.

He'd killed people.

He would kill more before this was out.

That wasn't what kept him up at night. No, his nightmares went back a lot further, and he had always held close the knowledge that he and his siblings didn't go after anyone who didn't deserve it. *Ryu* made sure of that with his research and hacking and compiling evidence.

He'd never seen Delilah coming.

Even now, even knowing she'd stolen his phone long enough to allow someone to hack it, he still wasn't convinced she deserved punishment. He simply wanted to know why.

Ryu guided the boat out of the bay and around the north side of the island. The west coastline faced the larger uninhabited island that they owned and used for various purposes. It also housed a handful of large villas for the clientele who wanted more privacy. Every one of those villas was outfitted with cameras and mics to ensure that privacy was only an illusion, but it wasn't something the Horsemen advertised.

People should know what they signed up for when they came to the Island of Ys. Having their every fantasy played out came with a price. If they weren't smart enough to realize that … Well, it wasn't the Horsemen's fault.

They kept one villa permanently empty in case they needed it, and that was where he headed. Unlike the others that were strung along the western curve, this one was tucked back from the coastline a bit, accessible by a hidden inlet that you had to know was there in order to find. He guided them into it and up to the dock that wasn't visible from the ocean.

It was only when he'd secured the boat that he spoke. "Do I have to carry you, or will you walk?" It came out rougher than he intended, but he was so fucking twisted up inside, he didn't have full control of himself.

He never seemed to have control when it came to Delilah.

"I'll walk," she said softly. She scrambled off the boat as if she wasn't sure whether he'd change his mind or not.

It stung.

Of course it stung.

He couldn't even reassure her that she was safe because she *wasn't* safe. Not on the island. Not from him. Not at all. Ryu kept his mouth shut and grabbed her bag, ignoring her attempt to pick it up. "Go."

Delilah looked like she might argue for a moment, but she finally huffed out a breath and marched up the wooden stairway to the main house.

This villa was smaller than the others, but it didn't lack for an understated beachy elegance that even Ryu found appealing. Normally. Right now, all he could focus on was the woman marching in front of him. He pushed through the large glass doors and held it open for Delilah. "Don't try to leave."

She ignored him and wandered deeper into the house. As tempted as he was to follow her, he had other things that needed his immediate attention. Ryu strode into the office situated in the back of the house and turned the computer on. He and his siblings rarely came out here, but he'd ensured it was stocked with a system that was identical to his in the hub.

His phone rang as he keyed in a few necessary software updates. Even without looking at the screen, he knew who it was. "Hey."

"Where are you?" Amarante sounded perfectly pleasant, which was a warning sign all its own. The more polite his sister got, the more dangerous she was.

"I had a few things to take care of, so I'm at our villa on the western side of the island."

"A few things to take care of," she repeated. "When you forced a week's waiting period, I didn't realize it was so you could take your woman on a honeymoon."

No point in defending himself. He couldn't without telling her the real reason he had Delilah out here, and *that* was out of the question. "You promised seven days. Where I am for the duration makes no difference."

Silence for a beat. Two. Finally, Amarante sighed. "I know you're upset with me, but—"

"Upset." He paced across the room and back. "*Upset* is when you pull some shit that goes over everyone's head, but it's for the best."

"Then why is this different?"

It was good they had a whole island between them. If they didn't, he might actually kick her ass. "We have one rule, Te. One. We look out for each other and we keep all four of us safe. There's no room in that for you sacrificing yourself. None."

"There's no other way," she said quietly. The utter conviction in her voice scared the shit out of him. Amarante was set on this path, and it would take a nuclear explosion to derail her.

"If you would have clued us in on what you were planning, we would have found another way and saved you scaring a decade off everyone's life. Since that isn't an option, you *will* give us seven days." He scrubbed a hand over his face. "And if you're thinking about pulling some noble stunt where you sneak off to do it anyway, know that we'll all come after you and then you'll be responsible for six deaths instead of just one."

"That's bullshit."

"So is your plan. Seven days, Te. Don't push us on this." Maybe he should have talked to the others before issuing this particular threat, but he already knew they were behind him on it. Maybe not their partners, but Kenzie and Luca would do whatever it took to rein Amarante in on this.

They all owed her too much to let her die for them.

They *loved* her too much to let her die for them.

Movement through the window drew his attention. The office faced the back of the house, where the jungle had been cleared back just enough to ensure that no one could approach unseen. They'd prettied it up with decorations and a winding flower bed, though, and as he watched, Delilah wandered down the rock path next to it.

Ryu waited to see what she'd do. There were no pathways through the trees back to the eastern side of the island, so she wouldn't make it far if she tried to run, but Delilah seemed the kind of person to try it if she decided it was her only course of action.

She studied the tree line before seeming to come to the only logical conclusion—that it was an impossible feat to get through—before turning back to the house.

Ryu took a slow breath and headed to the side door to meet her. She stopped short when she caught sight of him, but set her shoulders in a way he was coming to recognize. "So what's on the menu now? Torture?"

She had his hands effectively tied. He wasn't willing to actually hurt her, whether or not she'd accept that as truth. But he also couldn't let her leave. Not until he knew the truth. "Who did you hack my phone for?"

He hadn't thought it possible, but her expression closed down even more. "I don't know what you're talking about."

Ryu stepped back and let her walk into the house, but he followed her as she headed into the kitchen and rummaged around until she found the alcohol cabinet. A few seconds later she wrestled the lid off a bottle of tequila.

She took a long drink and finally looked at him. "So I'm, what, your captive?"

"Something like that." That's exactly what she was. Damn it, he should have thought this through better. But he hadn't been thinking. He'd only been reacting. It wasn't usually a weakness of his, but between his sister and Delilah, he'd had one mindfuck after another. "This would go simpler if you'd tell me what I want to know."

"Somehow, I don't find that remotely comforting." She contemplated the bottle and took another, longer, drink. "Let's play out this theoretical sequence of events, okay? Let's say I'm guilty. I confess, which makes me a traitor, and the Horsemen aren't known for dealing kindly with traitors." Another drink. He could almost see the alcohol hazing her vision now. "And if I'm innocent, I'll keep telling you that I'm innocent and you'll keep thinking I'm lying, and eventually you'll get tired of this song and dance and treat me just like the Horsemen treat a traitor."

"Delilah."

"No. Don't say my name like that. You don't get to basically kidnap me and then act like I'm being crazy when I respond in a totally understandably emotional way."

God, she was killing him. "I'm not going to hurt you."

Delilah turned those dark eyes on him and, suddenly, she

didn't look the least bit drunk. "Don't do that. Don't make promises you can't follow through on."

He opened his mouth to reassure her, but closed it, all those words unsaid. Because she was right. He couldn't promise her shit right now. He had no plans on torturing her, but he couldn't promise her safety.

"Yeah, that's what I thought." She hefted the tequila bottle. "I'm going to go to bed. When you figure out what you're doing with me, be sure to let me know." She wobbled a little as she strode out of the room.

She didn't look back.

* * *

DELILAH HAD to get out of here. Instead of the tequila relaxing her enough to sleep, it buzzed through her veins, demanding action. Stupid action.

She knew better than to get drunk, especially when everything hung on her thinking clearly enough to convince Ryu she was innocent. But she still hadn't processed the level of betrayal on both sides.

She stole his phone, yes. She'd even allowed someone to hack it, at least in theory.

Ryu *kidnapped* her.

Sure, he hadn't done anything particularly menacing since they'd arrived at this villa, but the fact remained—she wasn't free to leave. She couldn't get access to her phone, either, which meant she wouldn't be there when another call came through.

Esther was in danger.

There had to be a way out of this, and giving up wasn't an option. The last seven days had felt like an impossible time-line, but they were nothing on the *next* seven days.

She closed her eyes and pressed her hands against her

face. Even if she wanted to knock Ryu over the head and make a run for it, she wouldn't get far. Either the jungle would slow her down until he caught up, or she'd actually make it back to Pleasure, and then Death and the other Horsemen would stop her.

Delilah might have her doubts about what the hell was going on in Ryu's head, but even drunk as a skunk, she knew her options were significantly better with him than with the others.

So what to do?

That question drove her to wander the house, restless and too warm despite the air conditioning working overtime. She opened the fridge and let the extra cold air drift over her skin. It gave her two seconds of clarity, but it was enough to realize she had no business being outside her room until she had her defenses put back together again.

Stupid tequila.

She turned around, intent on heading back the way she'd come.

And screamed.

Ryu stood a few feet away, a strange expression on his face. The fact that there was any expression at all was a relief. He'd closed himself off to her. Not that she could blame him. She'd been lying in half a dozen ways since the start of this.

"Can't sleep?" His voice rumbled across the distance between them, and her body responded like a tuning fork. Her skin went tight and her nipples perked right up. *Stupid nipples.*

Delilah actually took a step toward him before she caught herself. "Something about being held in a house against my will doesn't pave the way for good sleep. Also tequila."

"Ah." Ryu leaned against the counter. Neither of them had bothered to turn on lights, but with all the windows and the half moon shining in, she could see him well enough to want him. But then, wanting Ryu had never really been the problem.

She should keep her mouth shut and go straight back to her room, but the night and alcohol loosened her tongue. "I wasn't faking it when we were together."

"I know." A wealth of knowledge in those two words. A reminder that he'd had his hands and mouth all over her, had seen her face as she came around his cock.

She shivered. What was she saying? Delilah licked her lips and drifted a step closer. "I should hate you for what you've done."

"Undoubtedly." Had he leaned forward? She couldn't tell.

The moonlight gleamed against his bare chest, tempting her to do the one thing she should absolutely not do. Touch him. Delilah's last step brought them nearly chest to chest. "Ryu, what are we doing?"

"Delilah." The way he said her name felt like he'd reached across the minuscule distance and run his hands all over her body. "Tell me the truth. No matter what it is, I can protect you."

She pressed her forehead to his chest and closed her eyes. With the alcohol fuzzing her senses, it was all too easy to believe him. She didn't want to carry this burden anymore. She desperately wanted to hand it off to more capable shoulders. Ryu might even be telling the truth. If she confessed, he would protect her.

He wouldn't protect Esther. He had absolutely no reason to. Even if he was inclined to try, whoever was on the other end of those phone calls had direct access to Delilah's baby sister. They'd hurt her before he could get there to save her. She wished with everything she had that there was another way. No matter how hard she concentrated, no alternative path opened itself to her. She was on her own.

He hesitated, but finally cupped the back of her head with

his hand, anchoring her to him. How could she feel comforted when he was part of the reason she was in this messed up situation to begin with?

She didn't know. She didn't care. She simply needed more of it.

Before Delilah could talk herself out of it, she lifted her head and went up on her toes to kiss him. Ryu's shock lasted half a breath before he lifted her and turned, setting her on the counter and stepping between her thighs. He cupped her face with his big hands and spoke against her mouth. "This won't fix anything."

"I don't care. I want you." Her life spun wildly out of control around her, and this man stood at the center, both the cause and the solution. If she was stronger, she wouldn't be pulling off her clothes, making little desperate noises as he skimmed his hands over her newly exposed skin. But Delilah wasn't stronger. She was scared and exhausted and the person partially responsible for that was also the only one she wanted comforting her. "Please, Ryu."

"As if I could deny you." He kissed her again, a slow, drugging kiss that left her dizzy and desperate. She reached for the band of his lounge pants, but he was already moving down to kneel between her thighs. Ryu pulled her to the edge of the counter and gave her pussy a thorough kiss.

Last time he'd gone down on her, he'd been in the mood to tease. He wasn't now. He fucked her with his tongue as if he couldn't get deep enough, as if he needed this just as much as she did.

Delilah clung to him, letting him hold her up as pleasure crashed through her. The sight of this man on his knees for her, the feel of his mouth on her, the thought telling her that this was a terrible idea … It all washed through her, driving her need higher. "My clit. Tongue my clit."

His rough chuckle vibrated through her and then he did

as she commanded, moving up to roll his tongue against her clit. She tried to hold out, to make it last, but Ryu wasn't messing around. He sucked hard on her clit and it was too much. She cried out as she came, digging her fingers into the counter and grinding against his mouth.

He barely gave her time to recover before he was on his feet. "Do you want my cock, Delilah?"

Was that a trick question? She nodded shakily. "Yes."

He guided her to stand and turned her around to brace her hands on the counter. The rustle of a drawer and a crinkle of foil and then he braced a hand on her hip and guided his cock into her. She closed her eyes. It felt too good. She wanted to soak up every second of this experience because all too soon they would go back to warily circling each other.

Ryu sank the last few inches into her, sheathing himself to the hilt. He lifted her hair off her neck and placed a kiss there. "You're safe with me."

No, she wasn't. She really, really wasn't. Not on any level.

He leaned over, his chest to her back, and ran his hands down her arms to lace his fingers with hers. "You are." He didn't give her a chance to respond—to *not* respond—because he started fucking her.

Long, steady strokes, letting her feel every inch of him. And, god, she loved it. She loved everything he did to her, everything they did together. A sound burst from her lips, half sob, half moan.

He took their laced right hands and guided them down her stomach to her pussy. "I want to feel you come around my cock. You clench me so tightly when you do. Like you never want to let me go."

I don't. Through some miracle, she kept those words internal.

They touched her clit together, the shared experience as

hot as the little circles Ryu drew with their fingers. He thrust deep, holding her pinned between his cock and his hand. "Fuck, Delilah. Look at us."

She followed his gaze to the glass doors leading out of the kitchen. In the low light, they were barely more than shadows, but as she watched, Ryu started fucking her harder, his larger form moving over hers in the image. "Turn on the light," she whispered.

He barely hesitated. Ryu reached past her to the switch on the wall and flipped it. Lights lining the bottom of the cabinets flared to life. It gave new detail to the reflection, and she moaned again. "We look good together."

"We look fucking *perfect* together." He released her hand. "Keep touching yourself."

He didn't have to tell her to keep watching them. She couldn't look away. She didn't want to. Ryu straightened and gripped her hips. He gave her one last slow stroke and then he picked up his pace. He fucked her like he wanted to imprint himself on her very soul. She could have told him they were too far gone for that, but Delilah was too busy stroking her clit, each of his thrusts pushing her closer and closer to another orgasm.

She met his gaze in the reflection and the sheer longing she found there pushed her over the edge as thoroughly as what he did to her body. She closed her eyes as she came, letting pleasure wash away her fear for a little while.

Ryu ran gentle hands over her body, easing her back to reality. He touched her like she was something to be cherished. Maybe even to be loved. Could he really lie that well? Or were these moments of softness the real man beneath the ice-cold exterior?

It was only when he pressed a kiss to her shoulder that she realized he hadn't finished. Delilah raised her head. "Ryu?"

"We'll talk in the morning." He kissed her neck. "Let me take you to bed."

Permission, then. A few hours of pleasure before reality came crashing back. Delilah hesitated, and finally nodded. "Okay."

He wasted no time picking her up and carrying her to his bedroom. They came together again and again through the night, as if he didn't want to leave this little pocket of peace any more than she did. As if he knew that dawn would bring back strife and put them back on the opposing sides.

It couldn't last.

She knew that, even as they collapsed beneath the first rays of sunlight edging through the window. Ryu pulled her against him, holding her tightly as if he could hold off what came next. He couldn't. He must have known as much, because his low words sent a chill through her. "You've put me in a hell of a position."

I don't want to do this. Can't we go back to pretending we're okay and the danger doesn't exist? Delilah cleared her throat and closed her eyes. No. There was no going back. They had to deal with this, one way or another. "Pretty sure that's my line. I'm the one who's playing captive. Except I'm not playing and this isn't a game."

Ryu let silence coat them for several long minutes, the only marking of the time passing being the tension bleeding into his body at her back. "I told you that I was hurt as a child."

The change in subject had her opening her eyes and rolling to face him. His expression gave her nothing, but had she really expected anything more? Delilah frowned. "You mentioned it." She'd figured the abuse had to be pretty intense to create such an intense trigger from being touched in that specific way. Delilah knew all about that, though thankfully she'd been able to dodge her own personal trigger

133

up until the last week. There was a reason she'd made it to twenty-six without learning to swim. She found herself holding her breath, waiting to see what Ryu would say next.

"The four of us found each other in a place called Camp Bueller. Two of my siblings were stolen and brought there. My sister and I …" His breath hitched. "It's recently come to light that we arrived there by different means."

She'd thought he was hurt by someone in the family or close to him. That was the usual path abuse took. A *camp?* She suddenly knew, beyond a shadow of a doubt, that she wouldn't like where this conversation went. There was only one reason children were stolen and brought to a *camp*. Her stomach lurched at the thought of the evil that must have gone on there. "Ryu," Delilah whispered. "You don't have to do this."

He ignored her. "Most kids barely lasted six months before they died or broke. My sister and I were there for ten years." Ryu shuddered. "Toward the end, I was on the verge of shattering, but Te kept me from crossing over. Barely. She couldn't save everyone, but she saved the three of us. I owe her everything, Delilah. *Everything*. It's not a debt any of us can repay, even if she won't acknowledge that it exists."

Oh no. No, no, no. "You think I have something to do with something threatening your sister?"

"I know you do." He touched her chin, bringing her face up so she had nowhere to look but directly at him. "I have a week to find a way to save my sister from a path that puts her in extreme danger, and I have absolutely no doubts that whoever put you up to trying to hack my phone is connected to the person responsible for Camp Bueller. My father."

The room gave a sickening spin. She jerked back, needing to put some distance between them. "What did you just say?"

"My father."

"Your *father* put you in that place?" Delilah's father might be as close to true evil as she'd ever come to, but even he had kept his violence to her and Esther. He hadn't spread it around. He hadn't profited from it financially. He still deserved to die in a ditch, but Ryu's father … She didn't know what the word was to describe something worse than evil. She didn't know if there *was* a word to encompass her horror.

Ryu rolled onto his back and stared at the ceiling. "I will protect my sister, and I will make him pay for what he's done."

The rest of what he'd said finally caught up with her. "Why do you think your—" She couldn't do it. She couldn't use the familial relation to describe that monster. Any connection to Ryu was too much. "Why do you think that man has something to do with me?"

"We're closing in. It stands to reason that he'd want someone on the inside to stop us before we truly endanger him."

She knew nothing about the man on the other end of the phone. He had no accent. No defining vocal characteristics. It wasn't as if he'd given her proof of identification before he started blackmailing her with threats against Esther.

Delilah sat up. She couldn't do this. "I …" She climbed out of the bed and bolted. She was almost to the doorway when her words got the best of her, too. "I understand, Ryu. Not about what you went through; I won't pretend our pain is anywhere near comparable. But I understand what it is to do anything—*anything*—to protect your sister." She didn't wait to see if he understood. She'd already said too much.

Instead, she ducked out of the bedroom and retreated like the coward that she was.

CHAPTER 13

 fter a morning spent coming to terms with everything Delilah had—and hadn't—said, Ryu knew one thing for certain. She betrayed him to protect her little sister. Whether someone had actively threatened the girl or had simply offered Delilah enough to make it worthwhile remained to be seen. In the end, it didn't matter. It was the one pressure point Ryu couldn't maneuver around. She'd fight him to a standstill and then keep fighting if she thought it would benefit her sister.

Just like he'd do for Amarante.

Which meant they were well and truly fucked.

He couldn't force Delilah to trust him enough to tell him the truth. He wouldn't hurt her or allow anyone else to hurt her, so she effectively had him over a barrel. Whether she knew it or not was irrelevant.

He also couldn't stop Amarante from going to the Warren to meet with their father. His sister would find a way no matter what obstacles he and the others threw in her path. His only hope lay in offering her an alternative way to kill their father that could be done without sacrificing herself in the process.

Ryu didn't *have* an alternative solution.

He sat back and stared at the monitors with all the information on Nicholai Krylov and the Warren. In the end, it wasn't much beyond what he'd already known. The Warren had been around for decades, though Nicholai had only taken over in the last ten years. He'd worked his way up from the bottom and he'd done it fast, resulting in the previous owner passing over several candidates to settle on him instead. No one knew where he came from before he appeared in the Warren, but everyone knew that crossing him was the last mistake a person would make. There wasn't a single instance of someone doing it and living. They all died eventually, and usually in terrible ways that served as a warning to others. It didn't matter how intensive their protective detail, how isolated their location; Nicholai always punished those who broke the Warren's rules.

Not even Amarante could get away with it.

Not even the Island of Ys would protect her if she did.

Ryu scrubbed his hands over his face and looked at the third monitor. It held everything he knew about Delilah and her sister, Esther. The file was significantly smaller than the one on the Warren and Nicholai. They were, by all accounts, two women who had seen some shit and come out the other side into something resembling a normal life. Her little sister was two years into a degree at Columbia. She kept her grades up, kept her nose clean, and showed all evidence of being exactly what she was—a college student intent on getting her degree and bettering her life.

Getting her degree that Delilah paid for by dancing at the club.

There was absolutely nothing to set them apart from thousands of other women on the same path ... except for the Island of Ys. He had no doubt that she'd been targeted for her proximity to the Horsemen—perhaps even him, specifically, because of his obvious interest in her.

"Fuck."

This was his fault, too. If he hadn't used Delilah's dancing as crutch, whoever this was would have passed her over without second thought. Her only value to them came because she could get close to Ryu.

He didn't know how to fix this any more than he knew how to fix the shit with Amarante. It made him crazy. Ryu dealt in *solutions*. But every time he turned around in this clusterfuck of a situation, something else popped up for him to trip over.

"Ryu?"

He looked up to find Delilah standing in the doorway. She wore a short robe that barely brushed the tops of her thighs and was a show-stopping red. It took far too much effort to drag his gaze to her face and stop thinking about what she did—or didn't—have on beneath it. "Yes?"

She wrapped her arms around herself, looking more unsure than he'd ever seen her. "We've known each other a week. Fewer than that, really if you count up all the hours. Would you trust someone with your sister's life that you'd only known that long? Would you *ever* trust someone else with your sister's life?"

He wished he could lie to her. If he was smart, that's the very least of what he should be capable of in order to convince her to tell him everything she knew. He wouldn't let emotions compromise his bottom line. Ryu looked into her dark eyes and couldn't dredge up a lie. "I've spent most of my life trusting only my siblings. Breaking that habit is damn near impossible."

"I thought so." She gave a sad little smile. "But that's exactly what you're asking me to do."

"That's what I'm asking you to do." He could use the fact that he never talked about Camp Bueller as leverage to demonstrate trust. It was nothing more than the truth, after all. Ryu *didn't* talk about his past unless he absolutely had to. He sure as fuck didn't offer up bits and pieces the way he kept doing with Delilah. She didn't know that, though, and telling her as much would only look like he was trying to manipulate her. Demanding her trust while offering no evidence to support his claim that he deserved it …Yeah, he wouldn't trust him if he were in her shoes.

The fact remained that he *needed* her to trust him.

He wished he could say it was solely for the mission's sake, but things had never been that simple when it came to Delilah, and it sure as fuck wouldn't be simple in this, either. She'd trusted him with her body time and time again, even after he proved he didn't deserve that trust. Selfish of him to want the rest of her, too.

Ryu didn't mind being selfish. Not now. Not in this.

He leaned back in his chair and studied her. "Let me ask you a question."

"As if I have a choice."

He pulled at the cuffs of his shirt. "What happens to your sister if you fail?"

"Ryu … Please, don't." She couldn't hide the fear tensing her muscles or the way her hands clenched at her sides.

Something bad, then. He'd known it must be, but this simply confirmed it. "If you had to trust her safety with me or with the person currently threatening her …"

Understanding dawned on her face and she gave a bitter laugh. "I have absolutely no reason to think that you'd keep her safe. None. Just because you like fucking me doesn't mean a single damn thing and you know it."

Her words stung. This *meant* something to him, even if she'd just been using him because she was forced into that position. The thought left him sick. Ryu scrubbed his hands over his face. "It means something to me."

She blinked. "What?"

"I want this to be real, not just because you had no choice." He gave a sharp laugh. "Fuck, that's an impossible thing to ask. I admire your survival instincts. I really do. Your sister is lucky to have you."

Delilah flinched. "It was real for me, too. It *is* real."

He barely allowed himself to dare hope she spoke the truth. There was no way to tell for sure without time to allow this to play out, and time was one thing they didn't have. He needed a solution, and he needed it now. "Your sister matters to you. Mine matters to me. That leaves us at an impasse unless we can work around it. I'm willing to try. Are you?"

"That's …" She lifted her hands and let them drop back to her sides. "You make it sound so simple. It's not that simple."

"It's exactly that simple." It wasn't. Amarante would balk at his diverting resources to handle this, especially if it came out that this was some mundane enemy and not their father. Ryu didn't care. He pushed slowly to his feet. "I give you my word that we'll try to save your sister, and that we won't hold her safety against you in the future."

Delilah crossed her arms over her chest. "Even if your word is good, it's an impossible thing to accomplish. It won't work."

He bit back a curse. "Delilah, I *know* you allowed them to hack my phone. It's not a mystery that needs to be solved. I also *know* that they're threatening your sister in order to get you to do what they want. The only thing your holding out is doing is wasting both our time when we could be finding a solution."

He picked apart her words, trying to understand. She sounded like she wanted to trust him. There was more than fear holding her back, though. Or, rather, more than a vague fear. "They're watching you. If you move out of turn, they said they'll hurt her."

She didn't answer, but her expression was answer enough.

"How are they watching you?" There was no such thing as a truly enclosed environment. Not even on the Island of Ys. They had the best security, they vetted their employees, and they did regular upgrades to ensure everything went off without a hitch.

They also invited the worst of the worst to frequent their location. As good as Ryu and his siblings were, they weren't infallible. Someone had found a crack and exploited it.

Delilah looked away and her shoulders dropped. "I don't know. They know things they shouldn't know, and it's enough."

He caught himself before he peppered her with questions. The fact she'd admitted this much was progress in and of itself. "You're safe here, in this exact place. There are no cameras in this villa and we're the only ones here."

"No cameras." She frowned. "How do you know that people don't wander through here whenever they want?"

He permitted himself a tight smile. "Because there *are* cameras set up around the perimeter. No one comes or goes without us seeing. But we're the only ones who use this place. We don't spy on each other." *Much.* Amarante always seemed to know things she had no business knowing. And Ryu had been known to check up on his siblings on the network that spanned both Pleasure and Pain. This villa was different, though. They came here when they needed a break but didn't want to deal with the security plans that came from leaving the island. It wasn't truly a break if meddling siblings were watching one's every move.

"Perimeter cameras. Of course."

A clocked ticked in his head, counting down the hours and minutes until this decision was taken from his hands. He didn't want to have to choose between Amarante and Delilah. He'd do damn near anything to avoid being put in that position.

How the hell was he supposed to convince Delilah to trust him?

He'd fucked that up from the very beginning, and nothing he could see of the future would do anything but make it worse. He leaned back and closed his eyes. If he were another man, the path forward would include seducing her. Things were so much clearer when they lost their clothing and their plotting and let nature take its course.

Ryu wasn't another man, and seducing her trust wasn't an option.

Unfortunately.

Fuck, what was he going to do?

* * *

TWO DAYS and Delilah had nothing to do but think. She worked out. She carefully tested the strength in her wrist. She ate and slept more than she had in weeks.

And she thought.

She meant what she said to Ryu. They'd reached an impasse she didn't see a way around. How could she? A sister for a sister. That's what was on the table. Either Esther or Death. As tempted as Delilah was to say fuck Death, she hadn't imagined the fear in Ryu's eyes. Fear for his sister and what came next.

Fear Delilah felt right down to her soul.

It had nightmares stalking her sleep, breathing down the back of her neck, whispering threats against the only person in this world she'd die for. Again and again, she woke up sweating and shaking, a scream trapped on the inside of her lips. The last time, she gave sleep up for a lost cause. She'd just have to take a nap in the afternoon like she'd gotten accustomed to doing. Delilah took a long shower, the hot water pounding against her skin banishing the worst of her shakes. It also brought things into glaring focus.

They couldn't continue like this.

Ryu had made it clear he would keep her here as long as he had to. Every day she spent away from the only way for her own personal nightmare to contact her, her anxiety rose. He said it would be another week, but she had no guarantees. If he called and she didn't answer, what would he do?

She didn't know. She just didn't know.

Thinking about it undid what little relaxation her shower brought. She stalked the dark halls of the house, not bothering to turn on any lights. No need when her wanderings had led her to memorize the layout and furniture placement. She took a turn to cross through the living room to the kitchen … And tripped when her legs encountered something that hadn't been there before.

Delilah fell with a surprised yelp, already bracing for the impact of the hardwood floors.

Instead, strong arms caught her, diverting her route. She landed sprawled on Ryu's bare chest. It took her brain several precious seconds to catch up and realize that they were not, in fact, injured. "What the hell?"

"You're welcome."

Fear and anger and something hot and slick had her sitting up and pointing a finger at his face. "I'm welcome? Are you kidding me? I wouldn't have fallen if you hadn't tripped me."

"I was sitting here, minding my own business, when you tripped. It's not my fault you didn't turn on a light or announce yourself." His hands fell to rest on her hips, a light touch that she felt right down to her soul. "I'm sorry, Delilah."

God, the thing the man could do with a handful of syllables. It simply wasn't fair. Her anger bled out of her, leaving only fear and desire in its wake. She leaned forward and rested her forehead against his. She was so incredibly tired. Bone tired. The kind of exhaustion that left her punch drunk and stupid. They couldn't go on like this. They flat out couldn't keep it up.

Words rose, words she had no intention of voicing. "You know, if things were different, I would be bending over backwards to seduce you into being my boyfriend."

His fingers flexed against her hips, ever so slightly. "If things were different, I would do my own bending for you."

"But they're not different."

"No. They're not."

Their breath mingled, their lips the barest hint of distance apart. She could kiss him now. It didn't have to be for a reason, or a plot, or some greater sacrifice. She could do it because she wanted to.

Because she wanted him.

Ryu's hands slid down to her bare thighs and then back up again, this time under her over-sized sleep shirt. His breath caught when he encountered no panties, and she almost smiled. She'd spent all her adult life creating fantasies for strangers, weaving the illusion of seducing them so they would throw money at her, and this man threatened to be undone by the least sexy thing she owned.

If things were different, she could love him.

If they weren't balancing on opposite ends of a conflict neither of them could compromise on.

The moment took on a dreamlike quality. She reached for him, withdrawing his cock and giving him a slow stroke. He dug into the side table and came up with a condom. Delilah took it from him, tore open the package, and rolled it over his length. A small movement, a tiny adjustment, and he was inside her. Even though neither of them spoke, this moment felt like a communion. A meeting of minds.

Pleasure built in slow waves, lapping against her resolve. She was so tired of standing alone. So tired of holding everything in and letting no one close. "Ryu …"

"Not yet." He smoothed his hands down her hips and around to palm her ass, guiding her movements, urging her closer and closer to the edge. "Trust me, Delilah. I've got you."

Words she wanted to hear more than anything in the world.

Delilah came in Ryu's arms with a soft cry. She kept riding him, kept drawing out the pleasure as he followed her to his own orgasm. And then he just … held her. Demanding nothing. Asking nothing. Just offering her comfort she most definitely didn't deserve.

She had to tell him the truth.

She *had* to.

"$\mathcal{I}$ got a call a little over three weeks ago from a phone that appeared in my bedroom."

Ryu stopped breathing. This morning he woke up with Delilah in his arms *again* and had vowed to find a way to make this work—to pave the way for many more mornings like the two he'd had here in this villa. He hadn't dared hope that she'd actually trust him enough to tell him the truth.

She shifted closer to him, her head tucked against his shoulder, her dark eyes hidden from him. "The man on the other end wanted me to spy on the Horsemen for him. I thought it was a joke or something. I mean, it was all very over the top. I told him to fuck off." Tension worked its way into her body. "The next day, I got a series of pictures of my little sister. They know where she goes to school, where she hangs out, where she *sleeps*."

He couldn't imagine the horror she felt upon seeing those pictures. The feeling would only be worse because she had no one to share it with. She'd been well and truly isolated.

No longer.

He pulled her closer and rested his chin on the top of her head. "So you agreed."

"So I agreed." She shivered. "Sleeping with you wasn't part of the plan. I thought I could dance for you and lift the phone, follow their instructions, and replace it."

An impossible task. Even as distracted as he was when she danced, he would have noticed. Maybe not right away, but it took at least a couple seconds to send and receive a text. "I would have caught you."

"You caught me either way." She sighed. "I was never much of a pickpocket."

"I could teach you a thing or two."

She lifted her head. "What?"

"We're hardly on the straight and narrow right now, but it still took a really rambling path for me and my siblings to get to this island. We stole, cheated, and played anyone we got close to for a few years there when we lived on the streets." Years during which Amarante had somehow managed to get her hands on a computer and a starting point for Ryu to learn.

Delilah frowned. "I tell you that I've been spying on you and your response is to offer to teach me to pick pockets better?"

"I already knew you were behind my phone being hacked. This isn't a revelation, Delilah." He smoothed her dark hair back from her face. "What I need to know is what happens next? He wasn't satisfied with the phone hack alone, was he?"

"No." She shook her head slowly. "He said I had seven days before he gave me my next instructions."

Time enough to ensure the phone hack worked, but the enemy would be a fool to pass up the opportunity Delilah offered. She'd gotten close enough to Ryu to be a threat. If circumstances were different, if they were different people, he might have been led around by his nose … right into the kind of trap a person didn't bounce back from.

"Do you know how he's monitoring you?"

"No. The phone showing up had to be left by someone, right? But he's known things that no one should be able to, stuff that happened when we were alone." She made a face. "At least I thought we were alone."

That was bad. Really bad. If it was simply the camera system they had access to, Ryu could find and eradicate them. A mole on the inside, though? That would be harder to determine, would take time they didn't have.

He set aside planning how to figure that out for a moment and cupped her face with both hands. "Thank you for trusting me."

"My sister's life is hanging in the balance. I … Please don't make telling you the truth be a mistake, Ryu." She worried her bottom lip. "He said if I so much as board transport off the island, they'll kill her."

"We'll find a way." He realized how ineffectual the words were the second he voiced them. Ryu cleared his throat. "You can't tell anyone what you just told me. Not a single one of my siblings." They wouldn't have the same restraints Ryu would when it came to dealing with Delilah's betrayal. "In the meantime, we play along."

She blinked. "What?"

"As far as anyone knows, we're here fucking each other's brains out."

That brought a small smile to her lips. "That *is* what we spent last night doing."

"We go back today. We act like nothing's changed. We keep up appearances." He took a deep breath. "With one exception. I have to tell Amarante."

"You just said you didn't want to tell anyone. Now you want to tell *Death?*" Real fear lurked in her eyes.

He wished he could expel it without lying. "If I don't give my sister a reason to hold off on her plans, then she'll be in serious danger. She might actually die. She'll do it for a noble cause, but that won't make her any less dead." Ryu took a slow breath. "I have absolutely no right to ask you to trust me further, but I need you to trust me to handle her and the situation."

Delilah pulled back, and he released her. She sat up and looked away. "And what about *my* sister?"

"I'll send Kenzie—War—to retrieve her."

She turned and stared. "Ryu, you said we'd keep it between ourselves and you just listed two out of three of your siblings as needing to be let in on the plan. I don't think secret means what you think it means when you put it like that."

Damn it, but she was right. And if Kenzie and Amarante knew, then Luca would have to be told as well. Ryu scrubbed his hands over his face. "You're right. Okay, change of plans."

"Uh huh."

"We'll go back. You'll go to your room. I'll deal with my siblings. Once I have them calmed down and reasonable, I'll get you and we'll keep up the charade for the rest of the public." At her skeptical look, he amended. "Public and private."

"We don't know how this guy is keeping track of me. Who's to say he won't have a way to monitor you, too." She shook her head. "Wait a minute, that doesn't make sense. If he could monitor you, he wouldn't need me. Forget I said anything."

Ryu carefully took her hands. He braced himself for the instinctive response to her palms against his, but …it didn't come. There was nothing but the steady warmth and the calluses from her work on the pole. He let loose a breath he hadn't even been aware he held. "I will do my best not to endanger you or your sister while I see this through. I promise."

She hesitated. "I suppose that's the best I can hope for."

"I'd be lying if I say there are any guarantees. There aren't. I suspect this person has some connection to my father, but I don't know for certain. Even if he doesn't, I'll make sure you and Esther are safe." It was the absolutely least he could do considering she was in this situation because of him.

"Ryu …" She stared at their linked hands. "I really, really want to trust you."

Easy enough to read between the lines. She'd had only herself and her sister to rely on for her whole life. It stood to reason that adding another person to the mix wasn't comfortable in the least. He brought their hands up and kissed her knuckles. "I will do my damnedest to be worthy of your trust, Delilah."

"Okay," she whispered.

"I need to make a few calls." He had to prep his siblings before he got back to the hub. With emotions running so high, he couldn't accurately anticipate how they'd react.

But it was a chance they had to take.

Delilah walked to the doorway, gave him one last searching look, and disappeared deeper into the house. He let out a slow breath, the weight of what he'd just agreed to threatening to grind him to dust. He couldn't guarantee her sister's safety. He couldn't guarantee *anyone's* safety.

Focus.

He headed into his office and made the hardest of the three calls. Amarante answered quicker than he expected. "Taking time out from your honeymoon?"

"Do you trust me, Te?"

She paused, as if he'd surprised her. "Of course I trust you."

"No, not like that. Do you trust me to make the right call? Do you trust me enough to give me the benefit of the doubt?"

This time, the pause lasted longer. "Why are you asking me this?"

Answer enough in that. He turned to look out the window. This place was supposed to be paradise—it *was* paradise—but sometimes he wondered it was all worth it. If they really needed to create a whole new sandbox to play in when they could have just as easily slid through the shadows surrounding their enemies. "I'm asking you this because I have information that potentially connects to our father, but it's sensitive and thorny."

"Thorny," she repeated. "This has to do with your woman."

No use denying it. "Do you trust me?" he asked again.

"Damn it, yes. Yes, I trust you." Real frustration leaked into her tone. "Do you think I *want* to go through with this risky of a plan, Ryu? I'm not so hellbent on this course that I'll turn away from an actual option."

He didn't really know if it was an option. Not yet. It would take most of the remaining seven days to hack his way through to figure out the person's identity. If they *weren't* connected with his father ... It didn't matter.

He'd promised Delilah that he'd take care of it, and he would. Regardless of the identity of their enemy. It wouldn't solve his fears for his sister, though. He pinched the bridge of his nose, fighting against the fear clawing through him. No matter which way he turned, he had no guarantees. None. If he didn't try *something* then Amarante would be in danger, and likely Esther as well. It didn't matter if they were connected or not.

"Ryu?"

He took a deep breath. "Someone is blackmailing Delilah

to try to get information on us. I don't think they intend to stop there, and I'm going after them."

"She told you this and you just …believed her." A world of censorship in her tone.

"Te," he warned.

"Do you really think that she's being truthful? Or is she simply angling for a permanent place at your side and she's using this fabricated danger to do so?" She laughed harshly. "*This* is what you wanted time for? I never realized you were so foolish when it came to women."

"Amarante, that's enough." He hated that she thought so little of him, but despite what she believed, his sister didn't actually know everything. "I have evidence that her claims are truth, not that I need to provide them to you. Even if I didn't, you acting like I'm a fumbling teenager who can't think past my hormones is bullshit. I'm bringing Delilah back to Pleasure. You will be kind and courteous and will refrain from threatening her. I need my main system, and once I have the identity of the man threatening her, we will launch a combination attack and rescue mission. And *then* we will decide how to handle the meeting at the Warren."

"It certainly sounds like you have it all planned out already."

"Either you trust me or you don't."

She sighed. "As you wish. Your woman will face no danger from me. You don't need my permission to allocate resources."

It wasn't quite the agreement he wanted, but it would have to do. "Thank you."

"Don't thank me. *My* timeline hasn't changed."

"Te—"

"I'll see you later today." She hung up before he could get another word out. His sister always had possessed a dramatic flair, though she kept it locked down most of the time. The ability to resist getting the last word was beyond her, though.

He ran his hand through his hair and braced himself for the next call. Kenzie was both more reasonable and more explosive than Amarante, and if she thought Ryu was being manipulated, she'd charge over here and handle Delilah herself.

In fact, maybe he shouldn't call her at all ...

His phone rang.

Ryu looked at it in horror. Damn it, he'd made a mistake, and he couldn't even dodge it because if he didn't answer, she *would* be out here inside of an hour. He bit back a curse and answered. "Good morning, Kenzie."

"You know, normally when someone seduces you just to spy on you, you don't bend over backwards to play into their hands." He wasn't fooled by Kenzie's teasing tone. She rarely telegraphed her intentions before she struck. "Honestly, Ryu, you're making us look bad. You're supposed to be the unflappable one and here you are, determined to get yourself killed. What is with you two?"

He strove for patience. "I see that you've talked to Amarante." In the last sixty seconds.

"Correction—I was standing next to her during that disastrous call. If your goal was to rile her up and make her even more determined to martyr herself ... Good job, you accomplished it."

Fuck. "I'm heading back to Pleasure shortly. I need you and the others to act like nothing is wrong."

She snorted. "Right. Like that's going to happen."

"Kenzie."

"Ryu." She mimicked his severe tone.

"I need you with me on this. Not just because of Amarante. I need you and your Irishman to take care of something off the island."

That perked her right up. "You always give me the best gifts."

"This one is a doozy. I'll tell you all about it—after you agree not to do anything rash when we get back to the casino."

She huffed out a breath. "*Fine*. I'll play nice with your little traitor. For now."

He wouldn't get any better offer than that. "See you soon." Ryu hung up and called Luca because if he didn't, then Luca would have to try to kick his ass on principle. He shook his head as his brother rasped out a hello. "I'm bringing Delilah back to the casino. Don't cause problems. Our sisters are doing enough of that for all four of us."

Luca was silent for a beat. Two. "Is there direct danger to us?"

"Not actively. I'm trying to deal with it before it escalates."

"Then I'll follow your lead. For now."

"Thank you." He set his phone down and exhaled the tension from his body. All in all, it had gone better than he expected.

Ryu went in search of Delilah. She didn't make it hard to find her. She sat on her bed, her packed bag next to her. Sitting like this, she looked …small. Breakable. It made him want to gather her up and stand between her and whatever sucker punches the world was determined to deliver. Ryu knew better. There were too many things he couldn't protect her from—couldn't protect *himself* from. "We'll get through this."

"You sound particularly confident of that." '

"We'll get through this," he repeated. Ryu held out his hand. "Come on. It's time to go home."

Delilah set her hand in his and allowed him to tug her to her feet. She looked at their clasped hands and frowned. "I forgot."

It took him half a second to catch up. He tensed and then slowly relaxed, letting the truth wash over him. She could touch him. He couldn't guarantee his reaction if she surprised him, but … She could touch him. He ran his free hand over hers, marveling at the strength and beauty there. "It's okay. You stopped being a stranger days ago."

"Thank you for your trust." She gave a bittersweet smile. "I really wish things were different. That I was just a dancer and you were just a guy. Maybe we could have made a go of things if there wasn't so much stacked against us. I really like you."

"I really like you, too." He gave her hand a squeeze and reached past her for her bag. This time, she let him take it without an argument. "There's no reason we can't make a go of it."

"You can't be serious."

"Why not?" He liked Delilah. A lot. Fuck, he might actually love her, though he'd be damned before he faced that emotion at this juncture. Not when they had so much in the air, so much that could go wrong. Those kinds of talk and commitments were better left for once the dust had settled. Once they were surer of each other.

But that didn't mean he wanted to let her cut off any possibility of it right now.

He held the front door open for her and then carefully shut it behind them. "I like you. You like me. We're about to run a gauntlet of trust issues that most people who date never have to deal with. Why *not* make a go of it?"

"Ryu …"

He waited. And waited some more. "Yes?"

Delilah nibbled her bottom lip. "I don't know. I was trying to think of a reasonable, responsible response and I got nothing."

"That answers that." He chuckled. Ryu led the way down

to the boat and helped her aboard. He didn't want to release her hand, but he could hardly get them unmoored and moving if he clung to her. Fuck, he was gone for this woman. He gave himself a shake and got to work.

It was only when they cut through the water around the north side of the island that Delilah spoke again. "No matter what you say, the other Horsemen won't want me here when this is all over. I've crossed too many lines."

She wasn't wrong, but Ryu didn't give a fuck. "You let me worry about it."

"Just like that?"

"Just like that." He slowed the boat and turned to face her. "You don't have to answer now, and we don't have to talk about it if you don't want to, but believe that I'm entirely serious when I say that I want more time with you." All the time with her.

Fuck, what was he doing? He couldn't say all these things to her, not when they were a single duplicitous week into … he couldn't even call this a relationship. Could he?

Delilah stood and pressed a quick kiss to his lips. "I can't promise that I won't overthink the hell out of this situation and the future, but I *do* want more time with you, too."

A warm feeling blossomed in his chest and he found himself smiling like the fool his sister accused him of being. Delilah wanted more time with him. He'd do whatever it took to ensure they got that extra time. He just had to remove the threat to her sister, convince *his* sister that there was an alternative route, and vanquish his evil monster of a father.

Simple.

CHAPTER 15

*D*elilah fully expected to be shuffled off to her room the second they got back to Pleasure, but Ryu claimed her hand and led her in the opposite direction. They walked through a door into a small hallway used by the staff to move through the casino. She knew the Horsemen kept rooms in the building, but they were strictly forbidden to anyone except the Horsemen themselves. She *didn't* expect Ryu to push a section of the wall halfway down and have it slide back to reveal a secondary set of halls.

He shot her a surprisingly boyish grin. "We like our privacy."

"Is that it? Or were you like every other child on the planet who wanted a house with secret passageways?"

His grin dimmed a little. "We aren't like every other child on the planet. We wished for simpler things." He tugged her into the hall and released her to trigger the door closing. "And, yes, we wanted a home with secret passageways."

"I knew it." She forgot, for a moment, what he'd gone through. In so many ways, Ryu seemed so … Normal wasn't the right word, exactly. He was a man who'd survived things she didn't want to think about too closely and then styled himself as one-fourth the Horsemen of the Apocalypse. *Normal* didn't come into the equation.

Then again, no one who worked and lived on the Island of Ys could be defined by that restrictive term. No, Ryu was simply *Ryu*.

And he wanted more time with her.

The cynical part of her wanted to believe he wanted more *sex* with her, but men like him didn't have to jump through these kinds of hoops to get laid. The sex was out of this world, but nowhere near enough to motivate him to put his neck on the line for her and Esther. No, he *liked* her.

The thought sent fiery butterflies soaring in her stomach. She liked him, too. More than liked him, if she was going to be perfectly honest. Delilah had edged right into infatuation. This should be a time for giddiness and letting her fantasies about the future have free rein. She'd never had that ability. Not when so much of her time and energy for the last eight years had been centered around making sure Esther wanted for nothing.

She sure as hell didn't have that option now.

Even if they managed to remove the danger, she couldn't see how this would work. No matter what Ryu said, Death wouldn't forgive this transgression. She might not send Delilah away, but she'd never give them her blessing. And Delilah would never put Ryu in a position where he had to choose between her and his siblings.

Her thoughts stuttered to a stop as he led her through a doorway and into a room that seemed to be a combination entertainment room, security room, and dining room. The hub he'd mentioned. For some reason, she hadn't expected it to *look* like a home. Even without windows, the warm cream walls and high ceiling gave the impression of space and lots of it. The large television took up the wall opposite the desks and monitors, and there were two overstuffed leather couches arranged in front of it that had to be expensive. The dining room table wasn't particularly large, but it was sturdy and made of shining dark wood. Four more doorways branched off from the main room. Those must be the hallways to their private suites.

Ryu's home.

Movement in one of the halls had his hand tightening on hers. Delilah's stomach did a low flip as Death walked into the room. She looked just as put together as she ever did, this time wearing a pair of loose slacks that flowed around her legs with every movement and a bright pink jacket-top that showed a deep V down her chest. Her hair hung loose around her shoulders in a perfect black river. She raised an eyebrow at them. "All my siblings have the terrible tendency to bring home strays."

Ryu half stepped in front of Delilah. "Be nice."

"That *was* me being nice." She cast a critical eye over him. "You look like shit."

"You've said it before. No doubt you'll say it again."

A small smile pulled at her pink lips. "No doubt."

Even sort of sniping at each other, the love between them was obvious. Delilah gave herself a full five seconds to let jealousy sting over the fact he got to see his siblings every single day. She hadn't seen Esther in months, not since she'd flown out to New York to surprise her for her sister for her birthday. She missed her, missed her in a way totally separate from the terror she felt over this whole situation.

Death turned those dark eyes, so similar to Ryu's, on her. In the space of a breath, she passed some kind of judgement, though Delilah had no idea what it was. The woman's expression gave away nothing. Death propped a hand on her hip and sighed. "I suppose my brother has promised to help you."

"I have," Ryu cut in.

She nodded almost to herself. "Then that's what we'll do." The woman waved a languid hand at the room. "Make yourself comfortable." Her gaze sharpened. "Though I think it goes without saying that I will happily make you disappear if you think to use my brother's kindness against us."

Ryu groaned, but Delilah lifted her chin. "I'm not going to betray you."

"You already have. If you do it a second time, you won't live to try for a third." She turned and walked back the way she'd come. A few seconds later, the sound of a door shutting softly nearly took all the bones out of Delilah's legs.

Ryu caught her around the waist as she wobbled. "Careful."

"Is it always like that with her?"

He cast a contemplative look at the doorway Death had disappeared through. "I wish I could say no, but most of the time, yes. People get used to it."

She didn't think she'd be here long enough to get used to it, but Delilah kept that to herself. She wasn't ready to burst what little bubble they had. Not yet.

Heels clicked over the tiled floor and Ryu cursed softly. "I'm sorry. I didn't know they'd ambush you like this."

She didn't get a chance to ask for clarification, but in the end she didn't need it. War strode into the room, a man at her back. Delilah got the impression of a nice suit and a dark glower from him, but then all her attention was taken up with the other woman. War wore a fitted red dress that hugged her body and left most of her legs bare. She also had a knife in her hand.

"Kenzie—"

"No. You do not get to *Kenzie* me." She pointed the knife at Ryu and then at Delilah. "And *you* don't get to fuck with my brother."

The man at her back rumbled out a laugh. "Put the damn knife down, Kenzie."

"You're supposed to be on my side!" She flipped the knife in her hand and passed it to him, handle first. Then she turned back to Ryu with a show-stopping grin. "Look at you! I'm normally the problem child and you've totally erased all the shit Amarante was annoyed at me for this week. I'm so proud of you." She pointed a finger at Delilah. "And you. I like you, but you break my brother, I break you. Got it?"

"Got it," Delilah said faintly. Being around the Horsemen was like standing in the middle of a hurricane. They each had such big personalities in their own way. She couldn't find her footing.

War gave her a brilliant smile. "Then we'll get along just fine." She propped her hand on her hip in nearly an identical way that Death had and frowned. "Ryu, for real, did you sleep even a little while you were out at the villa? You have bags on the bags under your eyes. Get a skin care regimen, brother."

"Kenzie," Ryu sounded like he wanted to throttle her. "I have things to do. So do you."

"Yes, yes, I'm getting to it." She waved that away. "We have a quick errand to run first."

Ryu used a hand against the small of Delilah's back to guide her out of the way. "Then get to it."

"Yeah, yeah." And then she was gone, trailing her man behind her.

"Come on. Let's get out of here before Luca decides to try some menacing of his own." He all but hauled her down the farthest hallway, and she let loose a laugh that had been building since the whole song and dance started. It was a little too hysterical to be comforting, but it was really the only appropriate response. Ryu stopped short. "Delilah?"

"Oh god." She slumped against him, giggling. "They love

you so much. I half expected one of them to start cleaning a shotgun like some overprotective dad."

He stared. "You ...aren't freaked out."

"Ryu, I'm so freaked out, I bypassed freaked out and am straight into whatever is on the other side of it. Your family is fucking scary, but I knew that before we ever had a conversation. You're the Horsemen, for god's sake. Your whole reputation is about being scary." When he kept staring, she felt compelled to explain. "Your sisters love you very much. Even though they're threatening me and would happily follow through on those threats if I step out of line, I'm just ..." She made a vague motion, not sure how to put it into words. "It's just so *normal* to threaten your little brother's girlfriend the first time he brings her home."

He nudged her through the door and closed it behind them. "I'm older than Kenzie."

That brought another laugh to her lips. It felt so *good* to laugh right now. "Sure, sweetie."

Ryu stopped short and seemed to really look at her. He gave a slow grin that had her stomach doing an entirely different kind of flipping. "Delilah."

"Yes?"

He caught her hips and tugged her closer. "You're my girlfriend."

Forget flipping. Her stomach was doing aerial spins. "What?"

"That's what you just said—they were threatening their little brother's girlfriend." His grin became downright blinding.

"You're impossible." She pulled back against him a little, but she didn't really want to escape. "That's not what I meant and you know it."

"Maybe ..." He shifted his grip on her and ran a hand up

her back, pressing them flush together. "But it could be the truth."

Her mind stumbled over itself in an effort to keep up with this turn of events. "You want to date me."

"I meant what I said when I mentioned a future. Yeah, Delilah, I want to date you." He leaned down until his lips brushed hers. "Want to go steady?"

"You don't think we should wait to make decisions like this?" She was grasping at straws and she knew it, but she couldn't seem to stop. It wasn't that she wanted to say no. She *didn't* want to say no. Fear had her feet rooted and her heart racing. She could barely think past all the things that could go wrong.

"Delilah," he murmured. "If we start running worst case scenarios, we're never going to live. This could all fall apart on multiple different levels. We don't know what the future holds. There are no guarantees."

"Are you trying to be comforting? Because you are not being comforting."

"My point is that why not grab for a little happiness while we have the chance? I'm happy when I'm with you." He paused. "Are you happy when you're with me?"

She closed her eyes, defeat and something like joy swirling through her. "Yes, Ryu, I'm happy when I'm with you."

"You want to be my girlfriend."

She rasped out a laugh. "Okay, yes, fine. I want to be your girlfriend."

"Perfect." He cupped her jaw with one big hand and tipped her face back to give him better access to her mouth. "Let's celebrate then."

"Ryu—"

Bang. Bang. Bang.

Someone pounded on the door behind him. Ryu sighed

and let his forehead rest against hers as he raised his voice. "What?"

"I have that information you wanted on the girl in New York." The speaker's deep voice was one she wasn't familiar with. "Stop making out with your woman and get your ass out here. Time's a ticking."

"Two minutes."

A laugh. "If that's all it takes, you better just start by apologizing."

He groaned. "Everyone thinks they're a comedian these days."

The obvious love his siblings had for him, the level of protectiveness they felt … It made her strangely happy. No matter how bad things had been when they were children, they had each other then and they had each other now. That kind of bond couldn't have a price put on it. "We should get to work."

"I know." He gave her one last fleeting kiss. "Rain check?"

"Definitely."

Ryu hesitated. "I wanted you to see the hub and meet my family, but we need to get back to the semblance of normality. At least for appearances' sake."

"Yes, agreed." She took a careful step back and smoothed her hands over her hair. "I'm going to talk to Laura about grabbing a shift tonight and getting back to work." They would probably be the last few shifts she'd ever have. Things would fall where they may in the next couple days, and no matter how they turned out, she couldn't shake the certainty that life would be forever changed.

Whether it would be changed for the better or the worse was beyond knowing.

"Good. We'll keep eyes on you and see if we can determine if the mole is electronic or an actual person."

"Okay." She hesitated. This might be the last she'd see of

him for hours …days. "I'm sorry about how this got started, but I'm not sorry for the time I've spent with you."

"I'm not sorry, either."

After that, there was nothing more to say. It felt a little like goodbye, but it wasn't forever. Delilah followed Ryu back into the hub and he led the way through a series of halls to a door that spit her out near the employee quarters. He gave her a long look. "I'll see you soon."

"Happy hunting."

She turned and walked away. It hurt. What a silly thing to feel right now. She had half a dozen world-ending fears hovering around her head, but all she could focus on was the growing distance between her and Ryu. It didn't seem to matter that she knew exactly where he would be, or that he obviously had every intention of seeing her sooner, rather than later. All that mattered was that they were farther from each other than they had been in days.

And it hurt.

She rubbed a hand over her chest, as if the ache were actually physical instead of all in her head. Was this what love felt like?

Delilah didn't know. The only person she'd ever loved was Esther, and that felt completely different. With her sister, it was part family bond, part almost parental. She cared for her, was proud of the strides Esther made over the years, felt joy over Esther's accomplishments and pain when she stumbled.

Yes, she missed Esther when they were apart, but they couldn't stay attached at the hip forever. She wouldn't clip her sister's wings just so she'd never leave. But it didn't *hurt* to be away from her.

Delilah stopped short.

Oh god.

She *did* love Ryu.

CHAPTER 16

*E*ven though Luca had interrupted them, he apparently decided he didn't need to give Ryu a talk about Delilah because they settled into work without so much as a hiccup. Luca went over the information they had on Esther and started putting together an extraction plan. Ryu started the slow process of combing over their security system.

There were so many moving parts that finding an intruder on the first pass was next to impossible unless they were an idiot. They'd managed to hack *his* system, so they weren't idiots.

Three hours later, he had a headache starting behind his right eye and a kink between his shoulder blades. And he hit pay dirt. "There you are, you son of a bitch."

"Tell me." He didn't jump when Amarante spoke at his shoulder. He'd felt her come up fifteen minutes ago. His sister liked to watch him work sometimes. She said the boredom of it relaxed her.

"They snuck in right after I changed the passwords last month. The reason I hadn't noticed was because they haven't actually touched anything yet. They're just piggybacking on our system." It meant they could see everything the Horsemen could on the island.

"Don't kick them out. It will tip them off that we're aware of their presence."

He barely resisted rolling his eyes. No shit, that would tip them off. "Given enough time, I can trace this back to its source."

"Don't bother."

He finally dragged his attention from the monitor to look at her. "What?"

"We know who's responsible. Which employee of his does the action makes no difference. It's our father."

Ryu had absolutely no reason to argue that. He wasn't even sure why he wanted to. "If I follow the trail, I can confirm for sure."

"It's a waste of time and resources." She turned away. "Go spend time with your woman. You won't have to play being lovestruck." She was gone before he could pick apart her tone to find the bitterness beneath.

Ryu pushed to his feet, but Luca's voice stopped him. "Don't chase her down right now."

He frowned. "I want to know what the fuck she's thinking that has *that* tone in her voice."

"You know what she's thinking." Luca kept scrolling on his computer. "She's thinking that she's scared about what comes next. She's both happy and sad that we've found people—that you appear to have found someone, too. Amarante has always set herself apart from us, at least a little. Now the divide is wider and she's feeling it."

He stopped and really *looked* at his brother. "That's some clear insight you have there."

"I've been sidelined for months, Ryu. You think I just sit around with my dick in my hand the whole time?"

It was more than that, though. Luca's fiancée, Cami, was off the island courting contacts in her home country of Thalania. Luca hated being stuck back here while she was gone, even though he had to know if there was one other place in the world where Cami was safe, it was in the palace with her brother, the king. Ryu chose not to comment on it. If his brother wanted to talk about it, he would. Instead, apparently he wanted to offer deep insight to Amarante.

"We're going to stop her from doing something fatal."

He typed something on the keyboard and sat back. "How?"

"What?"

"You heard me. *How* are we going to stop Te? Because you're fucking brilliant and Kenzie and I are no slouches. We don't have a solution, Ryu. We don't even have anything resembling a plan. Te won't stop for anything less than a fully fleshed out alternative option, and all we have is a vague 'later on, we'll get him.'" He shook his head. "She's going forward with it. You know it. I know it."

"No."

"Yes." Luca's expression seemed set in stone. "We need to stop wasting time trying to stop her from doing it, and start focusing all our energy on ensuring she makes it out alive."

"That's impossible." If it was anywhere else, they could manage it. Amarante would barely need their help. But the Warren had its reputation for a reason—it was why their father had chosen it, no doubt.

Luca finally smiled. "Since when has something being impossible ever stopped us?"

That was the question, wasn't it? He scrubbed his hands over his face. "We'll talk more about this later." After he had time to process the shift in gears. After he'd figured out how to extract Esther without endangering her further.

After.

Right now, he craved the peace Delilah brought him. It was more than that, though. Even when she aggravated and frustrated him, she settled something in his chest that he thought would be jagged for the rest of his life. He'd been broken a very long time, and the winding path to healing had caused parts of him to fuse together wrong. It was why he could function mostly normal, but couldn't stand strangers' hands on him. For so long, the only thing truly good in his life were his siblings. The strength of their bond held true as they all fought their individual paths back to the light—or at least some semblance of it—but it couldn't get them all the way there. Not after they'd lived in the darkness for so long.

With Delilah, he felt like he stood in the presence of the noonday sun. She warmed him just by existing, and when she turned her attention his way, it was like being lit up with fireworks. Amazing and slightly painful and something he wanted more of.

He loved her.

It didn't matter that it was too soon or that they had half a dozen potentially deadly problems between them and a happy, relaxed life. With each step that brought him closer to her, his worries took a backseat to sheer anticipation. Their few hours apart felt like years. He needed her, and he needed her now.

Except she wasn't in her room.

His phone rang as he headed for the main casino floor. "Yeah?"

"She's at the club."

Already? He glanced at his watch and winced. It was later than he'd thought, had definitely been more than a handful of hours since they parted ways. Of course she'd be back at work to keep herself occupied now that her wrist was feeling better. It *was* feeling better, wasn't it? Guilt flared. If she tried pole work before it was fully healed, she might injure it permanently.

His fault. Something he'd spend the rest of his life making up to her, even if she healed perfectly and it was no issue going forward.

Ryu changed course and strode through the halls to the club. Unsurprisingly, it was mostly packed at this time of night. Also unsurprisingly, his booth was empty. The manager, Laura, caught him before he walked three steps into the room. "We have your usual seat ready. Delilah is the song after next."

"Thanks." Seconds after he sat down, his drink appeared.

There was no relaxing on the menu tonight. Not really. His mind wouldn't stop racing even as his gaze lingered on the people occupying the tables around the stage and the dancer moving across it. There had to be a solution other than what Luca offered. They just hadn't found it yet.

They had very few days *left* to find it.

A slow song slid through the speakers around the room. Ryu knew it was her even before Delilah strode on stage. She looked just as beautiful as ever, her black hair wild around her shoulders and dressed in an outfit similar to the one she had on the night they first had sex. She paused next to the pole and cast a searching look over the room before she settled on him. With the stage lights, there was absolutely no way she could see him in the corner booth, but her brilliant smile sure as hell made it seem like she had.

He sat back and allowed himself to become lost in her dance. Before, he'd had the illusion that it was all in his head that she danced for him.

Tonight, it felt like reality.

Delilah inched her skirt down her hips in a sinuous move, working the fabric all the way to her ankles as she bent in half, facing away from the audience.

Ryu managed to drag his gaze from her and take in the people watching with rapt attention. Every single one of them wanted to tug her panties to the side to bare her completely. Every single one of them wanted to touch, to taste, to fuck.

Bastard that he was, he got off on the fact that he was the only one who'd be inside her tonight.

He swallowed half his drink in a single shot because Delilah had moved on to her top. She did something to the clasp that had it dangling from her arms and teased covering her breasts before she let it drop.

Then she danced before them wearing nothing but heels and her panties. Every bit of blood in Ryu's body surged into his cock. He hadn't thought she could get more attractive, but now he knew the exact sound she made when she orgasmed, and that she had a sly sense of humor even when fucking, and that her loyalty to her sister rivaled his to Amarante. It all came together into a woman unlike any other. One who seemed almost as if she was made for him.

Like they *fit*.

It would take him time to convince her of that. She'd suffered too much trauma over too many years to believe in happy endings that came without strings.

Hell, he had, too.

It didn't matter. They'd fight their way through her danger and then through his war, and they'd come out the other side to figure out what life without a threat hanging over their heads felt like. He had to believe that. He didn't have any other choice. They'd save her sister. They'd find a way to save his, too.

Her dance didn't last long enough, but that was okay. There would be other nights and more dances, both public and private. Ryu finished his drink, adjusted his pants, and headed for the private rooms. They were supposed to keep up appearances, but really he just wanted to see Delilah, to touch her, to reassure himself in the oldest way possible that she was okay. That *they* were okay.

She didn't make him wait long.

He'd barely settled onto the couch when she stepped through the door. Tonight she wore a deceptively simple lingerie set. A black bra offered her breasts up, the lace giving glimpses of her nipples. Her black lace thong gave the same peekaboo down below. Garters and thigh-high stockings completed the picture.

She took his fucking breath away.

Delilah smoothed her hands down her body. "You like?"

"I like you in everything."

"Good." She walked to him, a little swing in her step that had his cock jumping in his pants. She made to go for the stage, but he snagged her wrist and towed her close. "Let's start with a lap dance."

She raised her eyebrows but obediently straddled him, her body moving to the pulsing baseline of the song almost absently. "You look worried."

"I found someone has hacked our system and can access all the cameras."

She didn't so much as miss a beat. "So that's how they knew we had sex before."

He hated that she'd been put through that. Hated that someone had watched what they'd done without permission and tainted it. "I fully intend to make them pay for that."

"Good." She reached behind her back and unclasped her bra. No matter how many times she did this, no matter that they'd had sex now, his whole body went tight and the world stilled at the sight of her breasts.

"You're perfect."

Delilah laughed and caught his hands, guiding them to cup her. "This is against the rules but ..." She rolled her hips, rubbing herself against his cock. "Maybe we can fudge the lines a little bit."

Fuck, he wanted to. He wanted to so much he couldn't see straight. But he refused to put her in a situation where being with him would be used against her. Not Again. "The cameras."

"Oh. Those." She gave him a saucy smile. "I had them turned off before I came in."

That surprised a laugh out of him. "One could almost believe that you planned on taking advantage of me."

"That's because I am." She kept her hands over his, running them down her body and back up again. "I know we played pretend, but I want the real illicit fucking in this room with you." She released him and slowly undid the buttons of his shirt to push it aside. Ryu stroked his hands down to cup her hips, letting her guide them.

For now.

She quickly undid his pants as well and he lifted his hips so she could shove them down. Then Delilah just …looked at him. Like he was her favorite kind of candy and she couldn't decide where she wanted to start first. *"You're* perfect."

How could she look at him like that, knowing what she did about Ryu and his past? He didn't know. He suddenly didn't care. Delilah was a fucking gift, and Ryu would be damned before he did anything other than cherish her.

She pushed off him and slowly eased her panties down her legs. She'd put them on over her garters, the little tease, and so the black lace and tights framed her pussy once she moved to stand before him again.

As if Ryu could resist a temptation like that.

He pulled her forward and hooked one leg over his shoulder, opening her. This close, he could smell her desire, and it made him crazy. He dragged his tongue over her, savoring her. The moment seemed to stretch out, a bubble of unbroken time, but it burst when Delilah dug her fingers into his hair and towed him back to her pussy.

Ryu leaned back against the couch, bringing her with him, and licked her with the frenzy he'd had building in him since watching her dance. He needed her to come, he needed to be the reason she did, he needed to taste and touch and fuck until they beat back the lingering fear the arose when he thought about their future.

Delilah's cries mingled with the music as she rode his face with complete abandon. With complete trust. Her thighs locked around his head as she came, and Ryu didn't stop playing with her clit until she smacked the top of his head and he let her melt down his body.

He wasted no time pulling her close, rolling on a condom, and guiding his cock into her. It felt like coming home. Every. Single. Time. For a second, Ryu simply held her to him, as close as two people with different heartbeats could be.

She smoothed her hands down his chest and grinned. "I still can't get over being able to touch you."

"I like it." Especially like this, his cock sheathed fully inside her, her body wrapped up in his. Ryu kissed her as he began to move. Long slow thrusts as he took her mouth. Her tongue slid along his even as she lowered her hips to meet each thrust. Perfection. Everything about this moment, about her, was absolute perfection.

He leaned back so he could cup her breasts, playing with her nipples just the way she liked. "Everything about you is perfect."

She laughed, the sound low and infectious. "You're obligated to say that given our current activity."

"Doesn't make it less than the truth." He skated a hand down her stomach and circled her clit with his thumb. "I want to feel you come around my cock."

Her dark eyes went a little glazed. "Keep doing that, and you'll get your wish."

"As my lady commands." He didn't stop. The smooth roll of her hips went ragged, and he clasped her with his free hand to keep the rhythm. "That's it. Just like that."

She came. Fuck, but he'd never get enough of the wild abandon on her face when she orgasmed. He could spend a lifetime chasing this moment over and over and over again. Ryu hooked an arm around her waist and toppled her onto the couch. He took her mouth even as he gave himself over to the sheer joy of fucking her. Rough and wild and she clung to him, kissing him back just as fiercely.

I love you.

I know it's too soon, but I don't give a fuck.

I love you.

He managed to keep the words inside. Barely. Ryu orgasmed hard enough that the room spun slowly around him. He slumped down, the couch wide enough that he could wedge himself next to her instead of crushing her with his weight. "Damn."

"That about covers it." Delilah kissed his throat, his jaw, his mouth. "That was exactly what I needed."

He ran his hand over her hip, tracing the garter belt. "What time are you off?"

"Uh …" She snagged his hand and lifted it to look at his watch. "A couple hours."

He wanted to tell her to blow off the rest of her shift, but that was an asshole selfish thing to do, no matter how much he wanted to just be with her without all the other bullshit hanging over their heads. Ryu hefted himself back to a seated position, bringing her with him. "Stay with me tonight when you're done?"

Delilah smiled. "Why don't *you* stay with *me*? Just go to my room and make yourself at home. I'll be in after my shift."

It felt so ...normal ...to make arrangements like this. Wasn't it normal? He couldn't be sure. "You don't mind?"

"I kind of like the idea of coming home to you." She carefully stood and looked down at herself. She looked like she'd just been fucked, her brown skin flushed and her lips swollen from his kisses. Her pussy was ... *Fuck*.

He hooked a finger through her garter belt and towed her closer. "You have time for another private dance?" He cupped her pussy and pushed two fingers into her.

Delilah widened her stance, letting him fuck her slowly with his fingers. She arched into his touch. "I, uh, yes." She gave him a wicked grin. "But it'll cost you."

He leaned down and gave her clit a quick flick of his tongue. "Good. Because I'm not done with you yet."

CHAPTER 17

*D*elilah woke to the sound of ringing. She blinked into the darkness of her room, momentarily disorientated because she wasn't alone. She ran her hand down Ryu's arm where he'd draped it over her side, and he responded by cuddling her closer to nuzzle the back of her neck. She smiled despite herself. After the club, he'd come back here, and if her legs worked right this morning, she'd be really surprised.

The sound that woke her started up again. Ringing. She knew that sound.

Delilah shoved Ryu's arm off her and rushed to the dresser where she'd left the phone after they got back to Pleasure yesterday. He already knew what she'd done, so there was no reason to hide it anymore. She snatched it up. "Yes? Hello?"

"Bring Pestilence to New York within the next forty-eight hours or your sister pays the price."

Click.

She held the phone out, half certain that she'd imagined the whole thing. She hadn't. Of course she hadn't. When

Delilah recognized that they'd escalate, she hadn't anticipated *this*.

They wanted to kill him.

That's the only reason they'd use her to lure him out of
the safety of the Island of Ys. They wanted to take him, to
hurt him, to eventually kill him because no way would they
release him afterward. If she did this, she was accessory to
the murder of a man she cared deeply about.

If she didn't do it, they'd kill Esther.

Delilah braced her hands on the dresser and took several
gasping breaths. Oh god. They really wanted her to choose
between the man she'd gone and fallen for and the sister
she'd spent her whole life protecting. An impossible situation, even before she lost her heart to Ryu.

"It's okay." And then he was there, pulling her into his
arms and holding her close. "You're not doing anything I
didn't ask for."

She clung to him. She took the comfort he offered even
though she had no right to. "You heard?"

"I heard." He smoothed a hand down her hair. "I thought
they might try something like this. It's an opportunity."

"An opportunity," she repeated. "Are you kidding me?
They want to kill you, and because of your reputation, they
are going to come in with a small army or something. You
can't do that, Ryu. You *can't*."

"Delilah." He leaned back and brushed the tears from her
cheeks. She hadn't even realized she was crying and now she
couldn't seem to stop. "I won't go alone. I'm not about to play
the part of the sacrificial lamb." He made a face, and she
knew without a shadow of a doubt that he was thinking of
his sister and her plans.

That spurred her on. "Even if that's the case, you can't
leave the island right now. Not with Death about to do …
whatever it is that she's about to do. You need to be here for

her, not putting yourself at risk for me." She started to pull away, but his arms tensed around her. "I won't make you choose between us."

He looked down at her like he'd never seen her before. "You're not making me do anything."

"It doesn't feel like that."

He pressed a kiss to her forehead. It was sweet and reassuring at the same time, as if he really thought they'd find a way through this, as if his confidence was completely rock solid. She wished she felt the same way. The enemy had been several steps ahead of her this entire time. She had the utmost faith in Ryu, but he'd said it himself that he was distracted with worry for Death. Surely he wasn't thinking clearly.

"I'm afraid," she whispered.

"I'll keep both you and your sister safe, Delilah. I give you my word."

A hundred other fears bubbled up against her lips. They might deal with this enemy, but what of the others? Because there were others. The Horsemen had moved through the shadows too long *not* to make them over the years. The best case scenario was what? Letting Esther continue at Columbia until someone else figured out that her sister held a special place in Pestilence's heart?

She'd have a target on her back for as long as Delilah stayed here.

She'd have a target on her back for as long as Delilah stayed here.

Oh god.

Delilah rested her forehead against Ryu's chest. How was she supposed to tell him that he might not have to choose between her and his sister …but that decision lay in the balance for her with hers? She couldn't. Not now.

Maybe not ever.

Not when she knew exactly what his solution would be. Bring Esther to the island. Sure, it would keep her safe from harm for the time being, but it would be like putting a bird in a cage and expecting it to be pleased with this turn of events. Her sister was destined to fly. Delilah couldn't be the reason it didn't happen.

"Whatever you're thinking, we'll get through it."

The exact words she wanted to hear. She just wished she could believe them. "What if we can't? The deck isn't exactly stacked in our favor."

"Maybe not." He gave her one last squeeze and released her. "But we *will* get through it. Trust me, Delilah. Just …trust me." Ryu dressed in quick, economical movements. When she didn't immediately move to follow, he paused. "Now that we have a timeline, we need to get the plan in place. It's a little tighter than I'd like, but we'll make do."

Just like that. As if there wasn't a question in his mind that they'd save Esther and win the day. She walked slowly to her closet and pulled on a shirt dress that buttoned up the front. It wasn't fancy by any means, but she didn't want to face down Death and the others again in too casual clothes. A silly thing, maybe, but it gave her the illusion of a modicum of control.

At this point, she'd take what she could get.

Ryu took her on a different route into the hub this time. She'd known the "secret" hallways in Pleasure were extensive, but Delilah truly hadn't understood *how* extensive. She followed along, completely turned around. Her sense of direction didn't suck, but these seemed designed to confuse, especially when Ryu led her through a door into a closet and triggered something to have one of the walls opening into yet another hallway.

She shook her head. "This is exceedingly paranoid."

"We like our privacy." He closed the door behind her and

then took her hand. "Besides, you've dealt with our enemies. Do you really think these precautions are all that paranoid?"

If someone stormed the island and attacked Pleasure, they'd have to go through this maze of narrow hallways to get to the Horsemen. And the Horsemen and their people could launch attacks seemingly at random in a strange sort of guerrilla warfare. It sounded good in theory, but ... "What if they just decide to drop a bomb on you or set the place on fire?"

Ryu snorted. "Then we're in deep enough trouble not to worry about anything at all." He said it so casually, as if it was a risk understood and accepted.

"How do you live like this?" A couple weeks of intrigue and she felt bone-deep exhaustion that went far beyond the physical. How did he hold up under this kind of stress all the time?

He sobered. "We don't have any other choice." Ryu hesitated. "Actually, that's not the complete truth. We needed something to keep us going when we were young and trying to deal with all the shit that happened to us in Camp Bueller. The idea of melding into normal society was so foreign, we couldn't even comprehend it. I'm not sure all of us would have survived if we'd tried to go that route."

"Oh, Ryu." He couldn't possibly want her sympathy, but she gave it anyways. Delilah squeezed his hand and tried to keep her emotions locked down enough to listen without reacting too much.

"Amarante gave us a purpose, a route beneath our feet. We probably aren't the only survivors of that place, but we had her, and that was as good as any resource. We decided that we were going to make the people responsible pay and ensure what happened to us never happened to anyone else ever again." His gaze was a thousand miles—or fifteen years

—away. "This has always been my life, Delilah. I forget some-times that other people don't live like this."

What was she supposed to say to that? She didn't fault him for a single thing he'd done. He'd *survived*. That was more important than anything. She just …didn't know where she fit into his world. A dancer and the …whatever Ryu was. Hardly a crime lord. The Island of Ys was a perfectly legiti-mate business as best she could tell, though it wasn't as if she'd seen their books.

If he had a side plot to bring down someone who stole and abused children …

She didn't fault him that. Not in the least.

"Here we are." He led her through a doorway and back into the hub they'd visited yesterday. Famine was the only one present, and he looked exhausted. She knew something had happened to him—someone saw him brought in on a stretcher a few months ago and the gossip had run fast and fierce through the club—but he looked like he'd been put through the wringer. He'd lost weight and there were new lines on his face that hadn't been there the last time she saw him, when he was healthy.

For all that, he smiled at her in a way that was almost reassuring. "So you're the dancer that's got my brother twisted up in knots." He shot Ryu a look. "It's remarkably vindicating to see him lose his head after being so smug while I lost mine."

That's right. He and the princess were together. Or former princess? Delilah didn't exactly keep up on various countries' policy changes, but she thought for certain that she'd heard that the princess had been removed from the succession line.

Ryu shook his head. "As delightful as your amusement is, we have bigger things to handle right now."

Just like that, Famine lost his smile and became all business. He looked from Ryu to her and back again. "Did someone throw a wrench in our plans?"

"You could say that." He squeezed her hand, a silent sign of comfort. She appreciated that he kept it low key. She wished they were alone, because she'd tell him that she didn't need coddling. *He* was the one determined to put himself in danger right now.

Because of her.

She cleared her throat. "I got another call. They want me to bring Ryu to New York within the next forty-eight hours."

"No. Absolutely not." Famine turned to glare at Ryu. "Are you out of your fucking mind? They're not even trying to play coy right now. They aim to divide our resources—to divide us."

"I know."

She bit her bottom lip, hating the tension that rose between the two men. "I'm so sorry."

"Don't be sorry." Ryu pulled her close and wrapped his arm around her shoulders. "If they didn't use you, they'd find another way."

Famine ran his hand through his short dark hair. "They take out you, they remove one third of Amarante's protection for that fucking summit. Not to mention they *cripple* her."

She felt Ryu tense, even though no reaction showed on his face. "She'd be crippled to lose any of us."

"No shit." Famine waved that away. "I'm not playing who's the most important to our sister game. I'm stating a fact. They want her operating from a weakened stance."

Delilah looked up at Ryu. "You can't do this. It's too much of a risk."

"If I don't, they'll follow through on the threat to your sister. That's not an option. We'll take care of it, Delilah. There's absolutely nothing to worry about."

He was lying. She wasn't sure how she knew, but he *was*. Not about Esther.

He lied about it being nothing to worry about.

* * *

Ryu sent Delilah to his suite with a burner phone to call her sister. The second she disappeared, he turned to Luca. "Stop scaring her."

"I'm not scaring her. I'm speaking the truth." Luca shook his head. "This shit would be so much easier if we didn't have to worry about innocents being caught up in it."

"Delilah would do anything to protect her sister."

Luca raised his eyebrows. "Uh huh. And the only reason that you care about this college kid who has a target painted on her forehead because of us is because of Delilah. Sure." He motioned to the monitor behind him. "I don't like you walking into a trap, but it simplifies things."

"That's what I was thinking." He grabbed his chair and pulled it over to sit next to Luca. "We send Kenzie to grab the girl and I handle the guy threatening Delilah."

Luca shot him a look. "Correction: Cami grabs the girl, and the rest of us act as backup to ensure you don't get killed. We just have to convince Amarante to stay on the island until we get back."

Normally, he wouldn't worry about that part of the plan —Amarante rarely left the island—but with the decision about the summit hanging over all their heads, a niggling sense of unease filtered through him. "She has no reason to leave."

"As if that would stop her."

He cursed. "We get her word that she won't, even if we have to sit on her to accomplish it."

"Better." Luca nodded. "This is going to be messy no

matter how we play it. No doubt the asshole on the phone will set up a spot last minute, so we'll be scrambling to cover you, but we can handle it. We've made it work in worse situations."

"Not recently." They'd seen more action in the last three months than they had in years. He never thought it possible for them to become soft, but Luca's slip in Spain was enough to put a haze of concern over the whole situation. "We can't afford to fuck this up."

"I know." Luca hesitated, but finally clasped Ryu's shoulder. "We'll get the kid and we'll make sure we all walk out of New York intact."

Promises his brother couldn't make, but he accepted the words as truth all the same. Doubt killed in this kind of situation. They flat out couldn't afford to indulge in it. "I'm calling a meeting to lay this all out."

"Okay." Luca checked his watch. "Cami will be back in a few hours. I'll fill her in when she gets here."

Ryu nodded. It took less time than he expected to round up his sisters and Liam and pull Delilah from his suite. She looked like she was fighting off tears, but she didn't offer any information and he wasn't in a position to ask. Not when they had no time to talk about it. He guided her to a seat next to him and turned to look at his family.

It had grown. Something he'd been sure wasn't possible, and yet life had a way of surprising him. Ryu glanced at Delilah. There'd been a lot of surprising in the recent past. He finally understood what had turned his siblings' lives on their head when they met their person, though the path had been different for both Kenzie and Luca. No matter.

They had bigger issues to handle at the moment.

"The person threatening Delilah has given us an opportunity." He quickly went through what they knew and his plans to counter what was no doubt a trap. Amarante listened impassively. Kenzie looked about ready to jump to her feet and charge off to fight their enemies with her bare hands. Luca and he had already gone over all this, so his brother simply waited.

Amarante spoke first. "You want me to stay on the island."

"Yes." He met her gaze steadily. "And I want your word that you won't leave or do something impulsive while we're gone."

"You have my word."

He breathed out a silent sigh of relief. He truly hadn't expected her to agree so easily. It gave him hope that they could see this through and find a solution to keeping her safe. Time was the only factor holding them back. They went over the plan once more.

It wasn't nearly as fleshed out as he'd like. They were entirely too dependent on the enemy's timeline, but they had no other option at this point. Ryu would go to New York with Delilah under the guise of a romantic getaway. The others would travel with them in secret and wait for news of the time and place where Ryu would be taken. Meanwhile, Cami would get Esther out.

Ryu would have preferred Kenzie to handle that portion of the job, but Luca had a point about Cami being more than capable—and more likely to blend into a campus setting. Kenzie might have a slight advantage in the ring, but Cami could defend both herself and Esther without issue.

In the end, the meeting didn't take that much time at all. Kenzie, Liam, and Luca went off to get ready. Delilah took one look at Amarante and told him she'd wait for him in the hall. He watched her go, his heart in his throat. They'd make it through this and come out the other side safely. He had to believe that. To fear anything else was out of the question.

Ryu faced his sister. "I know it's not a good plan, but it's the best we have."

"We've made do with worse." Amarante sat with the stillness of a predator, but her expression didn't back it up this time. She looked almost …sad. "Be careful, little brother. I don't know what I'd do if anything happened to you."

"Probably burn the world down."

His joke fell flat when she nodded. "Probably."

"Te, promise me that we'll talk when I get back. I know you're determined to attend this summit shit, but it's a mistake. He's got dozens of people he could burn in order to kill you. There's only one of you."

She seemed to search his face, but he had no way of telling if she found what she was looking for. "Happy hunting."

He'd get no more out of her than that. Ryu nodded and headed down the hall to collect Delilah. They'd spend the night in her room and then fly out in the morning. The faster they got to New York and dealt with this mess, the faster they could get back to the Island of Ys and turn their attention to the bigger problem.

The future.

CHAPTER 18

*E*very time Delilah came back to New York, it felt like a slap in the face. The Island of Ys was hardly a lazy island life, but it had a certain relaxed pace that came from living in a community that encouraged every indulgence and hosted some of the most gorgeous weather she'd ever been exposed to.

New York's energy left her breathless. There were just so many *people*, all of them moving at a frenetic pace to get to their destinations. Between the lights and close buildings and constant barrage of sound, her senses screamed from the oversaturation.

It seemed impossible that she'd lived here for years before getting the job on the island.

It seemed even more impossible that she would come back here again to stay someday. Maybe sooner, rather than later. It wasn't like she could stay on as an exotic dancer after all this was finished. She was *compromised*, in more way that one.

Delilah gave herself a shake and followed Ryu through the

large doors into the hotel he'd booked. Unsurprisingly, it was expensive and luxurious enough to take her breath away. Ryu, naturally, didn't seem to notice. All the Horsemen were like that. They wore the most expensive clothes, moved in a world that was so far beyond the normal that it blew Delilah's mind and just … didn't notice. Or, more accurately, it seemed to fit. They didn't have to boast their wealth because they wore it like a second skin, as natural as breathing.

Her phone buzzed as she waited for Ryu to check in. Delilah's stomach dropped. No. It was too soon. They hadn't had a chance to get into position. *Nothing* was ready. She wanted to throw the cursed device across the room and then smash it to pieces for good measure. To scream. To do anything but dig the phone out of her pocket.

No choice. She hadn't had a single goddamn choice since the beginning of this, not when it came to keeping her sister safe. She lifted the phone to her ear with a shaking hand. "Hello?"

"Did you enjoy your flight?" He sounded as coldly amused as ever, as if he was in on some inside joke she had no part of.

Delilah looked at Ryu, but he was busy talking to the front desk guy. She took a slow breath and turned away from him. "I did what you asked. We're in New York."

"You know it doesn't end there, right?" He laughed. "I'm texting you an address. Be there at seven. You already have a reservation." He hung up.

The phone buzzed with an incoming text. She clicked the address and it brought up a location not too far from the hotel.

A restaurant?

She'd half expected for them to send her to some dark alley or the docks or wherever villains set up meetings.

Delilah gave a bitter laugh. She should know better by now. They walked around in the day like everyone else.

"Something wrong?"

She looked up to find Ryu in front of her. It was a token of her worry that she hadn't noticed him approaching. There was no telling who could be watching. If they arranged for a restaurant close by, they obviously knew she was staying here with Ryu. The lobby wasn't exactly crowded, but enough people lingered that she didn't want to speak plainly.

She tried and failed to dredge up a smile. "I was just thinking that it'd be nice if we went out to dinner tonight."

"Dinner," he said slowly. Understanding dawned in his dark eyes. "Dinner sounds nice." He held out his arm and she set her hand into the crook of it. "Let's get our stuff put away first."

"We can't take too long. We have a reservation in a little over an hour." An hour. The others were in the city, but she had no idea *where* in the city. The timeline would put Cami as intervening with Esther at nearly the same time they had dinner instead of hours before.

She didn't like it. She didn't like it one bit.

But Delilah held her expression as best she could and allowed Ryu to lead her to the elevator and take it up to their floor. A minute later, he shut the door to their room behind him. Ryu held up a hand, motioning her to silence. "Let's take a shower."

"A shower?"

"Yeah. Clean up after traveling."

She watched as he went into the bathroom and gave it a thorough search, going so far as to shine a light into the vent overhead. Finally, he turned on the shower and motioned her into the room.

Ryu shut the bathroom door. "We should be able to speak clearly in here if we're quiet."

"They sent me an address and made a reservation for seven. It'll happen there."

He pulled out his phone and started typing. "What's the address?"

She rattled it off, her heart in her throat. "This was a mistake. It's too fast, too soon. We'll find another way."

"No." He took her shoulders. "It's a tighter timeline than I'd like, but ultimately it changes nothing. We're going. It'll be fine."

It'll be fine.

Did he even *hear* himself?

She pulled away. "You don't know it will be fine. They might set up a sniper and shoot you from a distance. They might poison your food. There's a thousand ways they could kill you in a restaurant without stepping foot inside the building, and it doesn't matter if your siblings get the person responsible because you'll be *dead*."

"And your sister will be safe." He said it so calmly, it took several long seconds for the words to penetrate.

Did he just …

He did.

Delilah laughed bitterly. "So it's like that, then. You're still paying penance to your guilt and if this acts as punishment, then all the better." When he didn't immediately respond, she had to fight the urge to shake him. "You were so pissed at your sister for being determined to walk a dangerous road that could end up with her dead, and now you're here doing the exact same thing. What the actual hell, Ryu? Do you think your death will make up for anything your father's done? Because it won't. He'll still be a monster, and you'll be in the fucking ground."

"I don't have a death wish."

"Could have fooled me."

He pulled her close. She resisted for half a second and

KATEE ROBERT

then let herself slump against him with a muffled sob. Ryu wrapped her up in his arms and she could almost, almost believe he could keep the bad things at bay with nothing more than his formidable will.

Life didn't work like that, though.

"Ryu, I don't know what I'll do if something happens to you."

He hugged her tighter. "My siblings will be there. Nothing will happen to you or Esther."

Promises he couldn't make. He had no idea what would happen, so he had no idea if his siblings would be able to counter it. They didn't know *anything* right now. They were well and truly flying blind.

His phone buzzed and he released her with one arm to check the messages. His body relaxed against her, just a fraction. "Cami has eyes on Esther. She'll move on her the second we walk into that restaurant." Ryu gave her one last squeeze and released her. "It's time to go."

Words bubbled up inside her, panic and fear giving them wings. "Before we go … Ryu, I I—"

He pressed a finger to her lips. "Not yet. Tell me after we walk out of this unscathed."

That was the problem. She didn't know if they *would* walk out, let alone unscathed. What if this was her last chance to tell him that she loved him?

Delilah gave herself a shake. She couldn't think like that. Ryu already rode the edge of reason when it came to what might happen in the next hour. She couldn't afford to do the same. She'd have to believe enough for both of them. "Okay."

After that, they had nothing else to keep them from changing and heading straight to the restaurant. Every step of the way, tension knotted the muscles in Delilah's back. She *swore* she could feel eyes on her, but at this time of night, the sidewalks were crowded. It was impossible to tell if someone looked at them a little too long, or if they were being followed or *anything*.

No.

She couldn't panic.

If she did, Ryu would look after her instead of himself, and she needed him to be okay at the end of this. She didn't know what she'd do if he wasn't.

Their destination rose up in front of them all too soon. A classy restaurant with intimate low lighting and a classical feel. The hostess took their name and immediately led them back through the main room to a little hallway. "Our private dining rooms," she said as she swung open a door and motioned them in.

Delilah tensed, half expecting men with guns. But there was nothing out of the ordinary at all. Ryu held out a chair for her and then took the one directly next to her, leaving them both facing the door. He gave her hand a squeeze under the table. "Nice place."

How could he sound so calm when it felt like her heart might burst right out of her chest in fear?

"Ryu—"

"What are you hungry for?" He picked up the menu and started reading. The sheer strangeness had a hysterical laugh clawing its way up her throat, but she managed to hold it inside. Barely. Delilah picked up her menu with shaking hands, but the words blurred and ran together on the page. It was just as well. If she tried to eat right now, she might throw up.

She almost screamed when the waitress appeared, but Ryu seemed perfectly at ease. He ordered for both of them—a move she would have given him serious side eye for if she wasn't on the verge of losing it. The second the woman disappeared, he pulled Delilah out of her seat and into his lap. "Breathe. Everything is going to be okay."

"You can't promise me that."

"No, I can't." He rested his chin on the top of her head. "Have I ever told you about how my brother and Cami met?"

She knew he only wanted to distract her, but Delilah wouldn't hold off her fear forever if she just sat there and thought about all the horrible things that could happen to Ryu. "No, you never told me." She cleared her throat. "She participated in the Wild Hunt this year, right? They both did."

"That's right."

Now that he mentioned it, Delilah remembered a drama surrounding the whole thing. Normally War played the White Stag, the person hunted by the competitors. Catch her and they won—something no one had managed to do in the history of the Island of Ys. But this year, *Cami* had played that part. It had been all the gossip for the handful of days she managed to evade the competitors, right up until one of them caught her. Not Famine, though. He'd competed, but he hadn't won.

"Luca used to be a Thalanian noble, before he was taken." He trailed off for several long seconds, no doubt thinking about *who* was responsible for taking Famine—Luca. "He took one look at the princess and decided she needed someone to protect her."

Delilah pulled back enough to look at him. If this woman needed protecting, why the hell had they sent her after Esther?

Ryu nodded. "He went after her, planning to keep her safe. The first night, she ambushed him. She didn't really need his help. Not once." He tapped his pocket, the one that held his phone. "She accomplished what she set out to do."

Oh.

Oh.

She finally took a full breath and relaxed against him. So this story had a point, a secret meaning within meanings. Cami had successfully extracted Esther. Her sister was safe.

The knowledge should make her happy. Fear for Esther had been driving her for so long, especially in the last two weeks. Her relief felt hollow, like a breath she couldn't fully release. Even if Esther was safe, the danger hadn't passed. If anything, it was heightened now, because they'd have pissed off the people who wanted to use Esther as leverage. Ryu would pay the price if they failed.

She cleared her throat. "That seems uncharacteristically easy."

"I think so, too. She didn't see anyone watching your sister, and no one tried to stop her from hauling her out of her building." He frowned. "I fully expected there to be a fight."

She should be happy there wasn't, but she couldn't shake the feeling of another shoe about to drop. Nothing about this situation had been *easy* from the beginning. Surely it wouldn't start to go right now, when they needed it to the most.

The door opened and Ryu set her back in her chair. "Food's here."

"Sorry to disappoint, but there's been a delay." A blond man stepped into the room. He gave the impression of a Roman gladiator clothed in an expensive suit, as if the refinement was a costume he put on under duress when he'd much rather be wearing leather and wielding a sword. Delilah was barely able to adjust to his presence before he raised a gun and pointed it at Ryu. "I'm going to need you to come with me."

Delilah started to shove to her feet, but Ryu caught her arm and held her in place. He had a mild look on his face as if he'd expected exactly this to happen. "You're the mystery caller, I expect?"

"Someone's been telling tales." The man shook his head at Delilah before refocusing on Ryu. "I prefer Tristan."

She braced for that gun to turn in her direction, for the bark of a shot and the pain in her chest when the bullet penetrated. It didn't happen. Instead, the blond motioned with his free hand. "Come on, Ryu Zhao. I don't have all night."

Ryu jerked as if he *had* been shot. "That's not my name."

"Isn't it?" Tristan shrugged. "Have your identity crisis on your own time. I have my orders, and my employer isn't a patient man."

"No, I suppose he wouldn't be." Ryu rose to his feet and smoothed a hand down his suit. As if he wasn't being threatened right now. As if this was just a normal conversation and a normal inconvenience. He gave her a soft smile. "Go to our room and call my sister. She'll ensure you're taken care of."

Delilah stared. "That's it? That's all you have to say?"

The blond rolled his eyes. "He loves you. It's romantic. Let's go." He stepped back and motioned Ryu to precede him to the door.

She fisted the fabric of her dress, trying to resist the urge to start throwing things. To fight, to claw, to do *something* beyond just sit there like a target. "I suppose this is the part where you shoot me?"

"Why would I?" Tristan gave her a look like she was crazy. "You followed orders beautifully, dove. Your sister is fine, though frankly, she seems stressed the fuck out with finals. I doubt Death will thank you for leading her brother into a trap, but that's not my problem." He turned a sharp look on Ryu. "That's enough stalling. Let's go."

And then they were gone, disappearing out the door while Delilah sat frozen. Ten seconds passed, marked only by the racing beat of her heart.

Wait a damn minute.

What was she doing?

Delilah shot to her feet. She looked around, but there wasn't anything resembling a weapon conveniently stashed in the room. The closest thing she could find was a steak knife that seemed more for show than for function. It would have to do. She opened the door and slipped out into the hall.

It was deserted.

Delilah turned toward the main restaurant and changed her mind. The guy wouldn't have taken Ryu that way. There had to be a back door in this place, right? She headed deeper into the building, holding the knife at her hip.

As she turned a corner, someone grabbed her from behind. Delilah tried to strike, but they easily unarmed her and twisted her arm behind her back. Just as quickly, the person let her go. "Easy. It's just me."

Famine. Or rather, Luca.

She hissed out a breath. Thank god she wasn't alone. She didn't have the skills necessary to help Ryu now. His siblings did. "They took him."

"I know. Kenzie and Liam are following." He studied her. Somehow he looked bigger here than he had on this island, as if he'd shucked aside the inconvenient healing process while in enemy territory. "Are you okay?"

What a stupid question. Of course she wasn't okay. She'd been threatened, manipulated, and just watched the man she loved taken at gunpoint. She and okay weren't even on speaking terms. Yelling at Luca wouldn't help things right now, and having this conversation was only slowing them down. "I'm not hurt, if that's what you mean."

He nodded. "Cami got your sister. I'm going to take you to them now."

Delilah stopped short. "What do you mean? We need to go after Ryu."

"He wanted you protected, no matter what happened."

She wished Ryu was standing in front of her so she could smack him. She couldn't even be surprised that he made arrangements over her head to ensure that she was safe, even as he put himself directly in danger. Did he honestly think she'd abandon him?

Apparently he did.

She planted her feet. "Absolutely not. We're going after him." Delilah held up her hand to forestall any comments. "I'll stay out of the way, but he's got a better chance if you're there to help the other two."

Luca hesitated, clearly torn. "You will follow orders. No deviation."

"Yes. I promise." She had plenty of amazing skills, but none that would help in this kind of fight. Doing anything to jeopardize Ryu's rescue was out of the question.

He nodded. "Let's go, then."

She followed him silently, happy to be moving. Their path took them deeper into the restaurant and out a back door that led to the next street over. Luca checked his phone and took a right, setting a pace Delilah had to fight to keep up with. Through it all, her mind became a confused jumble of disjointed thoughts.

Ryu, Ryu, Ryu.

Why did Tristan let me go?

Oh god, Ryu, please be okay.

How do I explain this to Esther?

I don't know what I'm going to do if Ryu's hurt.

Hurt. She couldn't bear to consider an alternative. Surely if they wanted him dead, Tristan would have shot him in the private room and been done with it? She didn't know. She just didn't know.

Luca put out a hand to slow her. "They're close."

"How do you know that," she whispered.

"Can't you hear?"

Now that he mentioned it, she *could* hear sounds not too far in the distance. It took Delilah's brain half a second to understand what the sharp popping sounds were.

Gunshots.

CHAPTER 19

*R*yu had decided somewhere between leaving the private room and preceding Tristan out the back door of the restaurant that this was the best way to go about things. The man obviously had no intention of killing him yet, which meant he would take Ryu to the one person he both wanted and dreaded seeing.

His father.

He turned a slow circle, eyeing the buildings around them. His siblings were here somewhere, and he needed to call them off. It didn't matter if the thought of facing Fai Zhao after twenty-five years made his chest go cold. It had to be done. Better he do it now than let Amarante in a few weeks. He might not get out alive, but at least he wouldn't have Nicholai's hounds chasing him down if he did. Or that was what he told himself as a dark car slid up to the curb and Tristan nodded to it. "Here's our ride."

Ryu hesitated. "You know your boss likes to torture children?"

"I'm aware." Something went shuttered in Tristan's gray eyes. "I had nothing to do with any of that."

He studied the other man. Tristan was his age, maybe a few years in either direction. No, he hadn't been one of the people who frequented Camp Bueller. Could he have been one of the children, though? Ryu wasn't sure. He didn't recognize the man, but that didn't mean anything. "We want to stop him. Make sure that kind of thing doesn't happen again."

"If you're looking for a sympathetic ear, you'll have to look somewhere else."

He hadn't really expected it to work, but it was still worth a try. Ryu shrugged. "As long as you can sleep at night."

"I can't." Tristan opened the door of the car. "Stop stalling and get in."

Ryu took a step forward.

The glass in the back window of the car shattered. His body caught up before his brain did, instincts sending him to the ground even as he registered that someone had shot out the back window. Ryu lifted his head. "No!"

Whoever was behind the gun—probably Kenzie—obviously hadn't gotten the memo. Another shot, and the car lurched drunkenly forward until it hit the building. They'd taken out the driver. Fuck. There was no getting out of this rescue attempt now. He lifted himself into a crouch, still staying low to the ground, and turned to find Tristan pressed back against the wall of the restaurant. The blond looked really fucking tired. "Nothing ever goes to plan when it comes to your family, does it?"

"Now's the time to change sides." He didn't know why he said it. This man had terrorized Delilah for weeks on end and threatened her sister.

But he'd also turned around and walked away once she fulfilled her part of the bargain. That spoke of a thread of honor, which didn't match up with what Ryu knew of both his father and his father's operations. Who *was* this guy?

Tristan shook his head. "You should have come quietly. My people are in all the surrounding buildings. This will be over soon."

It would be over soon.

He meant they would kill Ryu's rescue party. His *family*.

He threw himself at Tristan, knocking the other man to the ground with a surprised curse. Ryu didn't give him a chance to recover. He punched him in the face, using the stunned moment afterward to go for the gun. A mistake, as it turned out. Tristan pulled a move that landed Ryu on his back. He started to surge up, but the cold press of metal against his forehead stopped him. Damn it, but he'd been fighting Kenzie for too long. She never would have managed that.

Tristan glared down at him, his gray eyes stormy. "Nice try, asshole."

"He's not the asshole." The voice came from behind them, and Ryu's heart actually stuttered at the sound. *Delilah*. What the fuck was she doing here, in what was essentially a kill box? God*damn* it. He struggled, but Tristan had him too effectively pinned. Movement in the corner of his eye had him turning his head even as he told himself not to. Delilah stood there, looking both terrified and determined. "Let him up."

"Somehow, I don't think I will."

A shadow fell across them on the other side. "Somehow, I think you will." Luca. He had a gun pointed directly at the other man's face.

Tristan sighed and straightened, lifting his weapon slowly and letting it dangle from his fingertips. Delilah darted in and snatched it, the gun appearing obscene in her hands. She didn't try to use it. She simply moved back into place near the wall.

"Up."

Tristan gave another sigh, like they'd just fucked up his day, and climbed to his feet. "This is a mistake. He only wanted to talk."

He.

Fai Zhao.

Father.

Ryu slowly sat up and then rose. "If that's the truth, there are a thousand better ways of getting a hold of me than playing the blackmail and kidnapping game." It wouldn't make a difference. *Nothing* would make a difference. Father or not, blood relative or no, he was the enemy. He'd committed too many sins to be pardoned, and somewhere along the way, it had become Ryu and his siblings' role to punish that evil. To put a stop to it for good. Nothing he could say to them would alter the path they'd set themselves on fifteen years ago.

All working to a final moment Ryu had hoped to spare his sister.

It wouldn't happen now.

He carefully took the gun from Delilah. "Are you okay?"

"I should be asking you the same thing."

He managed to spare her a smile that couldn't be reassuring in the least. Ryu turned back to Tristan. "Tell me why I shouldn't shoot you right now."

"Because my man has a line on your lady." He nodded, and Ryu followed his gaze. Sure enough, a little red dot appeared on her chest.

Fuck.

Ryu stepped in front of her, but it was a lost fucking cause. A bullet from a high-powered rifle would tear right through him and into her. He pointed his gun at Tristan. "Get the fuck out of here."

"You sure? Last chance to end this peacefully?"

He laughed. He couldn't help it. "Do you call *this* peaceful?"

Tristan shrugged and straightened his jacket. "I'm not talking about this. I'm talking about later."

Later. The summit.

He'd as much as admitted that Amarante was in active danger. Ryu had known, of course. If they planned to kill his father at the summit, surely the other side planned the same thing. But hearing it stated so baldly made the small hairs on the back of his neck stand on end. He caressed the trigger. "I could remove one enemy right now."

"Yeah. You could." Tristan shrugged again, as if he didn't really give a fuck. This man made no sense. "Your call, but clock's ticking. I don't walk out of here in thirty seconds, my man knows what to do."

He could put down this asshole. It would hurt his father's operation. They'd pruned his supporters too effectively, and Tristan running this operation on his own meant he was high up the hierarchy.

If Ryu shot Tristan, Delilah would be hurt.

She might die.

He couldn't be certain of the angle of the bullet, couldn't guarantee anything at this point. It wasn't worth the risk. Not to her. No matter what it meant for the future of the Horsemen's plans. He finally lowered his gun. "Get the fuck out of here."

"Wait." Delilah closed a hand around his arm. "What guarantee do I have that you won't pull this same shit again?"

"You don't." Tristan gave her a small smile. "But I'm not in the habit of wasting time and resources. You're burned as a contact, so why the hell would I bother to off some college kid? Not worth the effort it'd take to get to her."

Delilah frowned. "I don't get you."

"You don't have to, dove." He turned and walked away,

apparently unconcerned with offering his back to Ryu and Luca.

Ryu looked at his brother and shook his head slightly. They couldn't just shoot the guy in the back. They couldn't even knock him over the head and take him back to the Island of Ys, because there was the sniper to consider.

But.

He was alive. More importantly, *Delilah* was alive. He turned and pulled her into a crushing hug. "What the hell were you thinking? You could have been shot."

"*Me?* More like *you* could have been killed." She hugged him back just as fiercely. "God, I'm lightheaded."

"Let's get inside." He nodded to Luca, who fell into step behind them, still scanning for threats. Just because they made it out of that altercation didn't mean there wasn't more danger. He wouldn't breathe easily again until they were back on the island.

Ryu's phone rang the second the door closed behind them. He dug it out of his pocket while still keeping an arm around Delilah. He wouldn't be letting her go anytime soon. "Yeah?"

"Sorry." Kenzie sounded winded. "There were more snipers than we expected. I got four, but missed that last fucker."

"It's fine." And it was. They had accomplished what they set out to do. Esther was safe. The threat to Delilah had passed. He had no reason to believe Tristan would follow through on leaving her alone and yet ... His gut said the other man spoke the truth.

He really, really didn't get that guy.

Kenzie huffed out a breath. "You want me to go after the blond?"

"Yes." Now that they were out of the line of fire, if they

could go on the attack, he would. "Let me know when you have him."

"Your confidence is, as always, inspiring." She laughed and hung up.

Ryu didn't let go of Delilah as they strode through the building, back to the front and out the doors. A risk, this, but they couldn't stay holed up there indefinitely. A car veered out of traffic and stopped in front of them. The window rolled down and Cami grinned at them. "Did someone call for a driver?"

Ryu opened the door and all but shoved Delilah inside before following her. Luca hurried around to jump in the front seat. And then they were off, merging into traffic and moving away from the restaurant. From the attack. It took him half a second to realize they weren't alone.

Delilah let out a cry and threw herself across the seat at a younger woman who could only be her sister. They shared the same light brown skin and wave in their black hair, though Esther was built a little leaner than Delilah. She was also wearing a pair of sweats and a T-shirt and her feet were bare.

"Oh god, you're okay." Delilah gripped her shoulders and pushed her back to survey her as if she expected Esther to be bleeding from half a dozen wounds, and then hugged her tightly again.

"Yeah, I'm okay." Esther looked happy and confused. "Though this is the weirdest ass prank. You know it's finals week, right?"

"I know. I'm sorry."

He waited for her to explain what was going on, but she seemed to force herself to relax and sat back. Delilah gave a sheepish smile. "You know how I like pranks."

"When we were kids." Esther frowned. "What's going on?"

"Nothing," she said quickly. "You're safe. He's still in Texas. Everything is fine."

"Then what are you doing here?" Esther made a face. "Not that I'm not happy to see you, but it's kind of suspicious when a strange woman hauls me out of bed and basically drags me away, all while telling me it's for my safety." She frowned harder. "Delilah, what's going on? Don't lie to me."

"I, uh …"

Ryu wanted nothing more in that moment than to reach out and comfort her. She obviously wanted to shield her sister from the truth, and even if he questioned making that call, it was *her* call to make. He cleared his throat. "She wanted to introduce you to me."

"To you. Sorry to be rude, but who the hell are you?"

Delilah gave him a searching look, as if she couldn't understand why he'd put that truth out in the world. It struck him that she actually expected him to end things. He loved this woman, and she thought he had one foot out the door.

"Esther, this is …my boyfriend."

Suddenly, her sister seemed a whole lot more interested. "Boyfriend? For real?" She ran a critical eye over him, and Ryu couldn't escape the sensation that he'd been judged and found wanting. It was such a …mundane thing. To meet his woman's family. A privilege he never thought he'd have.

The fact they'd just come from a firefight and attempted abduction only made the whole situation that much more surreal.

"I guess he's cute," Esther said doubtfully.

"Thanks." Delilah laughed. "Ryu, this is my little sister, Esther. Esther, this is my boyfriend, Ryu."

Boyfriend.

He didn't think he'd ever get used to that label coming

from her lips, certainly not in connection with him. He liked it. He liked it a lot.

Esther yawned. "Maybe we can have like dinner or something tomorrow? I really do have class in …" She looked at her empty wrist. "In the morning."

"Right. Of course. I'm sorry." Delilah gave her a soft smile. "We were just in town for a few hours, but why don't I fly you out after finals are over? You can get some relaxation in and we can spend some time together."

Ryu couldn't quite catch his breath. Her words made it obvious she intended to come back to the island with him. He'd hoped, of course, but he'd barely dared dream it could be reality. Now that her sister was safe, he'd fully expected Delilah to pull the plug. How could she not when her very proximity to him made it possible something like this could happen again?

He sat back while they chatted on the way back to the college, trying to find a logical way forward. All the while, he kept his phone in his hand, waiting for a report from Kenzie and Liam.

Cami finally parked them near the dorms and Esther said, "This is me."

"I'd wish you luck during finals, but you don't need it. You'll kill it." Delilah gave her sister one last long hug. "Call me when you're done?"

"Sure." Esther gave Ryu one last long look and climbed out of the car. She paused and stuck her head back in. "Love you."

"Love you, too." Delilah waited for the door to close and then slumped back against the seat. "Is it really over?"

No. It was nowhere near over. They'd won a small skirmish in a line of small skirmishes, but the true conflict was yet to come. Pressure built around him, worry and stress and fear for the future. They hadn't found a solution to keep

Amarante from falling on her sword for them. "This part, yes." He hesitated, but the need to touch her, to comfort her, was too strong. "Come here."

She immediately climbed into his lap and clung to him. "God, I was so scared. I thought I was going to lose you."

He opened his mouth to tell her that she shouldn't have endangered herself to come after him, that she should have made a run for it, collected her sister, and gone somewhere safe. But all he could see was the evidence of what she felt for him. "You were magnificent."

His phone rang. "Yes?"

"The bastard slipped through our fingers. I don't even know *how* he did it, but he's gone."

He exhaled slowly. Not what he wanted to hear, but not unsurprising, either. "It's fine. We'll get back to the island and figure out how to handle the summit from there." Three weeks wasn't nearly long enough, but they'd make do. They always made do. "I'll see you back on the plane."

"See you there."

He hung up and slipped his phone back into his pocket. "Tristan got away."

"What does that mean for us?"

"It means he'll probably be at the summit Amarante is determined to attend in a couple weeks." Ryu didn't like that at all, but he couldn't argue that the man had a strange code of honor. "I think he meant what he said about you and your sister." A promise he had no business making, and yet …

He had a feeling it was the truth.

"I love you," she said it in a rush, as if she thought he'd stop her. "I wanted to say it before, but you were right. We needed to wait then … But I'm done waiting now. I love you, Ryu. I know this won't be an easy path, but I love you and I want to be with you. Just you." She straddled him and cupped his face with her hands. "I can't promise that it will be all rainbows and sunshine all the time, but I *can* promise you that I'll never lie to you again and that I'll be at your side no matter what happens."

It was more than he ever dreamed of experiencing. It took him two tries to find the words to speak. "You would be so much safer if you weren't with me."

"Haven't you figured it out by now, Ryu? Life isn't safe. Maybe for other people, but not for people like us." She smiled softly. "Do you love me? That's really the only question that needs answering."

"Yes. Of course. I love you so much, sometimes I think I'll drown in it." He hugged her close. This was happening. It was a fucking perfect moment in the midst of a nightmare. "Whatever happens next, we get through it together."

"Yes." Delilah kissed him. "Together."

CHAPTER 20

"I'm glad everything worked out like you hoped." Amarante latched her last suitcase and moved to the luggage cart just outside her room, her phone tucked between her ear and her shoulder.

"I would have liked to have Tristan to bring back to the island, but I suppose we can't win them all."

Tristan.

She certainly wasn't going to think about the fact *he* was the man behind this particular mess. No, she wasn't going to think about that at all. Her brother didn't know about her tentative connection with the man, and Amarante wasn't about to educate him. Not today. Not ever. "You did good, Ryu."

"I'm bringing Delilah back to the island." A hint of defiance in his tone. Even after all these years, her siblings continued to act like she was something set above them. Forever apart. Most days, they weren't wrong, but some days she wanted to claw and scream and rip down the invisible walls between them.

Too late for that.

Too late for a lot of things.

"I like her," she said. "I think she's really good for you."

He exhaled as if he wasn't sure she'd give her permission. "I love her."

"I know." Emotion clogged her throat, but she refused to let it through. It didn't matter that she felt like she'd lost her siblings, one by one, as they fell in love and their priorities shifted. She didn't begrudge them their happiness. It had become an asset knowing what she did now. In the wake of events to come, they'd each need an anchor. Their partners would provide that. They'd see them through to the other side, would ensure that they didn't buckle from the loss of her.

No use thinking about that. The time for thinking had long since passed. Now, the need to act propelled her.

"Anyway, we're about to take off, so I'll see you in a few hours."

"See you then," she lied. She hung up and allowed her shoulders to slump for the space of two breaths. Saying goodbye was never supposed to be part of the plan, but plans changed. She knew that better than anyone. She had a chance to end this for good, and she'd take it.

Better her than any of the others.

She scrawled out a quick note and stuck it on Ryu's desk as she passed with her luggage. She'd lied too many times in the last two weeks, but the price was worth it. Safety for her family at all costs.

That's why she hadn't told them that the summit wasn't in a month.

It was tomorrow.

Amarante took one last look around the room and closed her eyes. "Goodbye," she whispered. Then she grabbed the luggage cart and headed out of the hub.

She had a plane to Switzerland to catch.

* * *

THANK you so much for reading Ryu and Delilah's story! If you enjoyed it, please consider leaving a review.

Make sure to pick up HER VENGEFUL EMBRACE to see the exciting conclusion to the Horsemen's story! Amarante is determined to spare her siblings from any more pain, even if it means sacrificing herself to do it. The last person she expects to find at the summit is Tristan, the man who she might have fallen in love with if they were different people with different destinies. Will his presence be enough to derail her from her mission? Only one way to find out!

You can also pick up THEIRS FOR THE NIGHT, my FREE novella that goes back to where the Royal Triad of Thalania first began. An exiled prince, his bodyguard, and the bartender they can't quite manage to leave alone.

If you're craving something a little darker and a whole lot sexier, check out DESPERATE MEASURES! It's the first in a brand new series I fondly call Kinky Villains, and answers the question—What if Jafar won and he and Jasmine ended up together? Available now!

Want to stay up to date on my new releases and get exclusive content, including short stories and cover reveals? Be sure to sign up for my newsletter!

Join my Patreon if you'd like to get early copies of my indie titles, as well as a unique short story every month featuring a couple that YOU get to vote on!

ACKNOWLEDGMENTS

Thank you to Lynda and Eagle for saving me from myself when it came to polishing this book into something that shone!

Thank you to the readers who continue to put your faith in me and follow me along this strange journey. I love this series so much, and I'm so glad you do, too!

All my love to Tim. You know what you did.

ABOUT THE AUTHOR

New York Times and USA TODAY bestselling author Katee Robert learned to tell her stories at her grandpa's knee. Her 2015 title, The Marriage Contract, was a RITA finalist, and RT Book Reviews named it 'a compulsively readable book with just the right amount of suspense and tension." When not writing sexy contemporary and romantic suspense, she spends her time playing imaginary games with her children, driving her husband batty with what-if questions, and planning for the inevitable zombie apocalypse.

www.kateerobert.com

Keep up to date on all new release and sale info by joining Katee's NEWSLETTER!

Made in the USA
Monee, IL
25 January 2025

10929092R00132